PRAISE FOR BY WINGÉD CHAIR

"A wildly original and magical twist on the Robin Hood narrative, Kendra Merritt's *By Wingéd Chair* is packed to the spokes with complex characters, wry humor, and flawless world building."

-Darby Karchut, best-selling author of DEL TORO MOON and FINN FINNEGAN

"With a wonderfully crafted blend of swords and sorcery and characters based on Robin Hood, Merritt tops this story off with the lead character readers need nowadays; a strong, independent, powerful female mage who also happens to be in a wheelchair. Readers will be constantly turning pages to see what happens next to this fun group of characters through the twists and turns they won't see coming."

-The Booklife Prize

"Kendra Merritt's prose is fresh, with one-line descriptions that crack like a whip, and she doesn't miss an opportunity to surprise the reader. From the first line to the last, I was enchanted with *By Winged Chair*."

-Todd Fahnestock, best-selling author of FAIRMIST and THE WISHING WORLD

Mark of the Least Series

By Wingéd Chair

Skin Deep

Catching Cinders

Shroud for a Bride

A Matter of Blood

After the Darkness

The King in the Tower Collection

Daybreak Colony Duology

Surviving Daybreak

Daybreak Sentinel

Mishap's Heroes

Magic and Misrule

Death and Devotion

Trust and Treason

Illusions and Infamy

Sparks and Scales

Wastelands and War

Eldros Legacy

The Pain Bearer

After the Darkness

Mark of the Least

KENDRA MERRITT

BLUE FYRE PRESS

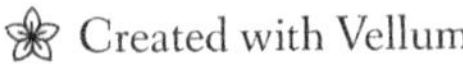 Created with Vellum

This one's for Dad, who shows the world what drive and hard work can do.

I promise I'll write you one with ships soon.

CHAPTER ONE

It has been two hundred and ninety-six days since the Darkness lifted. The mighty Vemiir Empire that once stretched from coast to coast, across the great northern mountains, and bridged the channel to the south now lies in ruins. The great towers of Leu'aline lie scattered across the plain.

Like every other constant in my life, it crumbled to dust. My family, the only thing I have left, surrounds me with their love and their misunderstanding acceptance. They shelter and care for me, but they do not understand me. They do not know what I went through. What I lost when the Empire fell. No one does. No one but another magi would. And as far as I know, I might be the last of those.

Months ago, I found this journal in the ruins of my home, and now I think I finally have the courage to write about what has happened. Do I imagine someone in the far future will read my smudged and illegible account? That seems like the same hubris that condemned all of civilization. But at this point, I can do nothing else. I am good for nothing but to set *pen to paper and tell my story to what little remains of the world.*

I set down the stick of sharpened charcoal and stretched my fingers. It had been months since I'd made them do anything so tedious as write. We hadn't been encouraged to record our thoughts or trials in the Forge. Retrospection wasn't necessary for Tempering.

"Aurelia," my sister, Claudia, said. "Come sit by the fire and stir this pot. It's going to stick otherwise."

I rose and tucked the book and my makeshift pen into the threadbare satchel at my waist. Our shelter for the night had once been a sprawling country villa with orchards and outbuildings. Now, barely two stones stood on top of one another, and we sat in what was left of the kitchen, waist-high walls keeping the dark at bay while the roof opened onto the sky.

Claudia took my elbow and ushered me to a seat on the stone block beside the fire, which crackled in what had once been the hearth. I wanted to snap that I wasn't an invalid, but I didn't have the energy after weeks of constant travel. And if I snapped at Claudia, I would have to find ways to rage against all of my family because she wasn't the only one to treat me like glass. Or even the worst one.

Fine lines of power drifted from the verdant greenery around us, flowing almost like water. Claudia puttered around the pot as if they didn't exist while I squinted and tried to see around the wisps of light. At least they were starting to gather in little pools and streams. When the power had first appeared, the wisps had been so ubiquitous they'd looked like a blanket of blinding energy covering the world.

Claudia knelt beside the fire and fed it more wood—pieces of furniture this time, an elegant chair with whorls and curling leaves carved into the surface, now dry and cracked from lying in the sun for most of a year.

Claudia was the best at this mundane skill. I could light the fire with a thought and keep it burning through the night with hardly anything to feed it, but I couldn't stand the way my family looked at me when I did so, with that mixture of horror and awe and now and then a little pity.

Before the Darkness, they'd sent me off to the Forge with hope and laughter and so much love. But everything had changed, and this thing they had all wished for now made them jumpy.

A footstep thudded on the cracked flagstones beyond our shelter, and Claudia reached for her short sword, propped unsheathed beside the fire.

"Are you going to gut me, sis?" a voice said, and my brother, Max, poked his head over the broken wall that sheltered our fire. He grinned and sat on the stone to swing his legs over into our campsite.

Claudia scowled. "Could you be any louder? We heard you coming a mile away."

"But did you hear *me*?"

Claudia and I both jumped and then laughed as Papa stepped out from behind us. The light of our fire glinted off his silver hair, turning it gold. He wore the simple leather of a foot soldier. His parade uniform had crumbled to dust along with the rest of the Empire, but I would always think of him in the gold and red, like an angel in the temple of the Allfather.

He let his hand rest on my shoulder, and I sat up straighter.

"What did you find?" Claudia asked. She had coiled her long blonde hair around her head and somehow gotten it to stay. The ladies of Leu'aline had used magic to keep their hair in place. Before the Darkness had taken that from us as well. I had to remember to ask her how she did it. I could only braid my dark hair and tie it off with a spare piece of leather.

Papa and Max emptied out their sacks as Claudia and I marveled over their treasures.

Dried, wrinkled apples came out first and Claudia cried out and snatched them. "They're perfect." She swept in to kiss Papa on the cheek. "Thank you." Then she hunched over the pot with her knife and tossed chunks of fruit into our cook pot.

I winced. I didn't really like the way everything went into one pot and came out looking like something from the wrong side of Leu'aline's cuisine district. But beggars couldn't be choosers, and what we scavenged went further when it was boiled.

Max produced a sack of grain which went over almost as well. Claudia had once been the quartermaster for an entire division of the legion, and she often joked that cooking for our family was nearly the same thing.

Papa sat beside me, and I tried to smile at him. He looked so much older than when I'd left home, older even than when he'd pulled me out of the pit in the Forge. It wasn't that long ago that his hair had been the same color as Max's and mine. The first and last of his children, we'd been the only ones to inherit the darker shade.

"I found you something special," he told me.

My smile turned real. How many times had Papa come home from a campaign and said those same words to me?

He reached into his sack, like a street magician, and pulled out a gown the color of sunflowers.

My mouth dropped open in appreciation, and I reached to touch the soft fabric. It didn't fall apart at my touch.

"Where did you find this? How is it still intact?"

"I think we were in the old servants' hall. One of them must have had a penchant for permanent things. Or a father who was a legionnaire."

I snorted ruefully. "Not every legionnaire's daughter learned to make clothing the hard way." I certainly hadn't. Mine had all been held together by magic. Just like almost everyone else in the Empire.

"Take it," he said. "The rest of us are comfortable in uniforms. But I know you're not."

I let the fabric slide over my hands, a decadent luxury I hadn't known how much I missed. Mixed feelings crept up my throat. The uniform they'd found me fit just fine, but I hadn't earned it like the rest of my family. Even Mamma had been a legionnaire when she was younger. I'd been set aside for the Forge, so I'd never served.

But donning a different set of clothing when my entire family wore the branded leather would just make me stand out more. They'd only have to look at me to remember our differences. If they ever forgot them at all.

Still, Papa gazed at me, eyes crinkled with fondness and soft with regret, and I wanted so much to erase the latter. Nothing that had happened had been his fault.

So, I gathered up the folds of fabric and limped off into the ruins of the house to find some place private to change.

By the time I returned, the rest of the Namarus family had gotten back from foraging. It was a good thing the villa's kitchen had been so large. It was the only place all of us could rest in the same space.

Mamma joined Claudia at the cook pot, her fair hair cut so short it curled around her ears. They argued over the best way to make the stew go further, adding some flour, using a little of our precious dried meat, maybe a little more water. Papa had taken charge of the boys and oversaw their efforts to erect a canvas roof over a corner of the kitchen. Max laughed while the twins, Quintes and Valens, struggled with the supports to hold the canvas in place. Decima was supposed to be on mending duty tonight, but the pile of uniforms lay forgotten beside her as she sharpened the two short swords she normally wore strapped to her back. My aunts argued about the arrangement of bed rolls while my little cousin scampered between their feet. And Granmamma had appropriated the only intact stool, presiding over it all with a fierce grin.

I loved the chaos so much it hurt. It was good to see everyone with a smile or a joke on their lips. We'd spent too many weeks walking, too many months searching for food, water, and a place to rest. The villa was the first place we'd felt safe in a long time.

Every single one of them looked up when I stepped into the firelight, and they shouted greetings.

"Aurelia!"

"Aurelia, you look beautiful," Mamma said. "Yellow suits you."

"Hey, Papa, would you find me one, too, next time?" Decima said.

Quintes squinted at her. "What do you need a dress for? It'd be like wrapping a scarf around an ax handle."

Decima, who wore her hair even shorter than Mamma and compared her own nose to a knife edge, threw a chunk of rock at Quintes.

I rolled my eyes and picked my way across the kitchen to sit at Granmamma's feet. I eased my left leg along the ground, stretching the sore muscles. Mamma spared a warm smile for me, but she remained at the cook pot with Claudia so she could oversee the distribution of bowls and cups. We'd found enough in the ruins of the kitchen that everyone could have their own. A new and appreciated luxury since we'd been sharing three bowls between the twelve of us since we'd left Leu'aline.

I dug into my sludgy stew as everyone else settled on the flagstones, ignoring how it tasted and the fact that dried apples floated alongside beans and oats. It would make my stomach stop moaning, and that was all that mattered.

Decima took her bowl with her to stand watch outside the circle of firelight.

"This is nice." I used my spoon to indicate the villa. "Almost...almost like home." It was a dangerous sentiment for everyone, but the barest sliver of contentment had wormed its way into my mind and infected everything else.

Mamma reached over to pat my knee like she understood what I was trying to say. "It is nice to finally be sitting still."

"We could stay here," Aunt Iulia said, watching her boy play with two spoons he'd found in the wreckage. "It's secure enough, and we could forage in the orchard and glean from the fields until winter."

Max shook his head, his overlong hair falling in his eyes. "It might look nice, but where are the walls? The watchtowers?" he said. "I don't like how open the fields are." He was a soldier first, but he'd served with the legion's engineers long enough to have a good eye for building.

"But those same fields could feed us," Aunt Priscilla said. "Couldn't we grow new crops?" She'd trained recruits in sword and bow work. Farming was completely new, but at least she was willing to learn.

Claudia said, "Yes" at the same time Max said, "We should move on."

Quintes surveyed the ruins with his nose wrinkled. "We could try to reach Icthein," he said. "At the very least, there will be fishing. And winter should be milder there."

Papa's lips thinned. "Without magic for the supports, Icthein will have fallen into the sea by now. If any of the city remains, it will not be a safe haven but a death trap."

I lowered my gaze as if I were to blame for the magic failing and an entire city sliding into the waves. Granmamma placed her gnarled hand on my head.

No one questioned Papa's declaration. Granmamma had been a legionnaire longer, but she'd retired too many years ago. Her knowledge would be skewed by time and the expansion of the Empire.

But Papa had spent forty years spear-heading that expansion and knew the Empire better than anyone. He'd helped conquer the northern province above the mountains where there was nothing but ice and barbarians and two other provinces after that.

"What about Alta'ine?" Claudia said. "It's defensible, and its fields were large enough they can't possibly be picked over by now."

Even Papa stopped to consider her suggestion. But finally, he shook his head. "It's still the remains of a city. Those who survived the fall will be living in its ruins, and we are too few to carve out a place among them." Papa stood and turned to survey the villa and the night surrounding it. Everyone waited, eyes on him.

"This is a good place," he said. "Better than any we've found so far. We can make it defensible." He met Max's gaze. "And I don't like how close winter is getting. We'll stay here."

"We'll make it work, then," Mamma said.

A collective sigh moved through my family, even from the ones who had been arguing. Even if anyone wanted to disagree, we were too tired. Magi had once moved armies from the mountains in the east to the west coast in a matter of hours. I don't think any of us had had a proper sense of the immensity of the Empire until we'd tried walking across it.

Or I should say former Empire. We'd given up on finding any of our society intact after so long. With so many of our councilors kept alive by magic, I doubted any of them had lived through the Darkness. Without them, only people like Papa would care to keep the world together.

The whistle of a night bird pierced the dark, and every member of my family straightened. It was a well-rehearsed signal from Decima.

Papa flowed to his feet, his hand resting comfortably on his hilt while the rest drew their weapons and moved into defensive positions around the fire. Even Granmamma stood, drawing a short, curved bow from the shadows beside her seat.

I drew my own knife, but Papa's hand slashed through the air to point toward the middle of the group. My shoulders jerked, but I followed his orders. As a legionnaire's daughter, I could defend myself, but I didn't have the training the rest of my family had, so I was lumped in with my little cousin.

With Decima's warning, it seemed like we had forever to prepare before they attacked. Almost twenty fighters surged over the walls into the firelight, their surprise telling us clearly that they'd thought to take us unaware.

If they'd come to our group with sheathed weapons asking for help or to share our fire, my father would have done his best to meet their needs. But this way...

Papa drew his sword as the first came over the wall, and he ran the man through with little preamble. Then the rest of my family moved.

I loved watching them. It could have been a court dance the way they turned and spun and kept track of one another. My three brothers spread out and overwhelmed the enemy one at a time. Claudia charged headfirst into the fray while Decima flanked our attackers and whirled in to take three of them before they even knew she was there. Beside me, Granmamma took careful aim to cover each of them.

Papa engaged a large man who wore the remains of his clothes tied around his waist. As soon as he was distracted and overextended, Mamma dove in with her knife. My parents worked as a team in all aspects of their life, not just hearth and home.

We were unstoppable. Nothing would threaten us.

Then ten more came out of the dark carrying swords and pikes stamped with the crest of the legion and that was too many.

This was the largest cohesive group we'd seen out in the wilds of the fallen Empire. And they swarmed over my family.

I cried out as Max went down and Claudia took a blow to the head. Papa spun to look, and his enemy took that moment to grab Mamma.

Bile stung my throat. I wasn't a warrior, but I could see the turn of battle as easily as any general. In a moment, we would be lost.

The light glowing at the edges of my vision snapped into lines and flowed in spirals, centering on me.

The man standing over Claudia raised a club studded with bits of glass, ready to bring it down on my sister.

With a wordless scream, I drew the lines of power in, gathering it as a ball of burning light only I could see. Then I flung it out into the enemy, and it roared through flesh and bone.

The man clutched his bleeding chest, grasping for the

weapon that had stabbed him. His fingers found nothing but blood, and he fell heavily to the dirty flagstones.

One by one, they toppled. Ten of them. Magi before me had slaughtered whole divisions, but only those that had been trained in battle managed that kind of power.

I sagged under the weight of my ineptitude, falling to my hands and knees.

The rest of our attackers stopped and stared at their fellows, the marks of death seeping into their makeshift, threadbare clothing. My family scrambled to regroup in the lull. They fell back to form a tight circle around me, dragging the still forms of Max and Claudia with them. Mamma stomped on her captor's instep and twisted away from him.

The man let her go and his eyes swept over my slumped form, looking for the telltale blue, but my clothing had been left behind in Leu'aline.

"Magi." He spat the word as if it tasted like ash. He and his men still hesitated like they were trying to decide whether to kill me or flee.

I climbed back to my feet and tried to look like I could do whatever I'd done again.

The man's lip curled. "Magic scum." He spat on the ground and pointed his sword at Papa. "We kill every magic user we find. It's no less than they deserve."

"That's funny, considering you tried to kill us before you saw me." My voice came out steady even though my hands still trembled with fatigue.

The man sneered and addressed my father as if even looking at me would contaminate him. "We'll be back with three times this number to take care of her." He raised his chin and stalked off into the night, taking his brigands with him.

"Do you think they have that many?" Quintes asked as Mamma and Priscilla knelt to check Max and Claudia.

"It's more than we've seen working together anywhere else," Granmamma said.

"We're not risking it," Papa said. "Even if they don't have the numbers, they can tell anyone they meet they've seen a magi. We'll have to fight anyone who wants to take their anger out on a magic-user. Our best bet is to disappear from this place. Pack up."

No one complained, even though ten minutes ago we'd decided this would be our new home. The villa had seemed so perfect.

"I just—" I said, but I didn't know what to finish it with.

Papa spared me a smile and a touch on my hand, but that didn't change the fact that we were fleeing because of me.

My jaw clenched, and my fingers curled into fists at my sides. Standing in the center of their circle, letting them defend me had made me feel fragile. Like they thought I needed protecting. But that wasn't it.

I was dangerous. A weapon, cocked and ready to go off, and the moment I did, I'd bring my whole family down with me.

The only way to stay safe was to bury the weapon as deep as possible and guard it against anyone who might set it off.

CHAPTER TWO

I don't want to dwell on what I went through in the Forge. I
don't think it's necessary, but Claudia has pointed out
that with the world gone, there will be people growing up soon
who don't know how magi are Tempered. She's right,
damn her.

The Empire was built by magic. Magic made the soaring
glass towers of our cities possible; it kept our councilors alive
long after they would have died of old age; it even held our
clothes together. There was no shortage of power. Only a
shortage of those who could use it. And the Empire had had a
thousand years to refine ways to make magi, a process that
eventually resulted in the Forge.

After so long, the Forgers had it down to a science. They
knew what bloodlines, what pressures would make a magi.
They even had a word for it. Tempering. A man or a woman
would come to the Forge for Tempering and they would leave
a magi. They were so good at it their failure rate had dropped
to five or six individuals a year.

Of course, the only reason that number was so low was because the Forge only took people they knew they could Temper. They had studied the bloodlines. They knew which families were most likely to produce magi.

Over a thousand years, those families had risen to power and prominence in the Empire. Families of magi quietly ran the world. Everyone else had to work up to it the hard way.

Papa was the youngest general ever promoted by the Empire. In his time, he conquered three different provinces, and the last was enough to get him recognized by the Commissioner. But not enough to get him into the higher courts. Papa might have been instrumental in gaining those provinces, but he would never have any say in how they were ruled.

Unless one of his children became a magi.

After years of service, countless strings pulled, and favors called in, Papa was given one chance, one opportunity. One of his children could be accepted into the Forge on the off-chance that they could be Tempered. And I, as the youngest of the Namarus family, was chosen.

I'd been born with one leg shorter than the other. Not a great hardship in the splendor of the Empire, but it was clear, I'd never serve in the Legion. So, I was set aside for a better use and as such I was the culmination of my family's years of experience and education.

It's not an exaggeration to say the Forge had Tempering down to a science. Applicants from an established family went into one program. The tried-and-true program that produced magi like little souvenir figurines, perfect and identical. Those few of us accepted from elsewhere were placed in an experimental program. It meant we went through everything the normal magi went through, plus more when that failed to work.

A person requires two things to work magic: bloodline and hardship. For the first, certain families produce more magi than others, just like certain families all have red hair or cleft chins. And just as those features can pop up out of nowhere in families that haven't seen them before, so too can magi. But since it's far more likely to see magi come out of the known families, the Forgers concentrated on them.

For the second, the magi's ability to work magic is the body's response to trauma. Life threatening, life changing trauma.

I knew this going in. I'd accepted it as the price I paid for my family's honor. For the reaction to occur and Tempering to be complete, the brain must not just think it's in danger, it must know it. So, the Forge created situations to convince the brain it was about to die.

And after a thousand years of studying how magi reacted, the Forgers were experts at trauma.

Papa's brilliance might have helped expand the Empire, but in this new age, I just appreciated that he kept a map of it in his head. We moved from one possible settlement to another, always searching, always analyzing, with one thought driving our feet onward. Home. Home. Home.

All we'd found so far was wilderness and ruins.

Here, in the center of the Empire, most people had lived in the soaring cities. But those definitely weren't safe anymore with their toppled towers and the survivors scavenging through the wreckage. Forts were a much better option. The legion always built with mundane means, since magic was too easily sabotaged by the enemy. Which meant they might still be intact after the Darkness.

But there weren't as many of them in the heart of the Empire. We had to keep walking farther and farther from the cities to find anything that hadn't been built with magic. The villa had been our best option in months.

Sourness pooled in my stomach, making me grimace. I had to keep reminding myself the world was dangerous now. My family would have been out here searching for a safe haven even if I'd died in the Pit. And knowing them, they'd have encountered just as much trouble without me. Just different kinds of trouble.

Every day I kept my head down, ignoring the lines of light and the wash of power across my skin. That was a piece of me that caused more trouble than it was worth, and I fought it down, shoved it away, locked the trapdoor, and pulled the rug over it. For the sake of my family.

We all wanted to find a place to call our own. But I wanted to be sure I didn't get them killed along the way.

I'd been given the task of watching over Granmamma as we traveled. Max said it was because I was her favorite. But I knew it was just to keep me busy. Granmamma was the toughest of all of us. More often then not, she was the one helping me clamber over rocks with my uneven gait. The lifted boot on my left foot helped me keep up with the hard pace, but I was still sore in the evenings.

Over rolling hills, through little pockets of forest, across miles and miles of grassland. I got really tired of grass.

A week's travel from the abandoned villa and months after we'd left the heaping remains of Leu'aline, we crested a hill to find the endless expanse of green and gold grass broken by a broad strip of water glinting in the sunlight. It curved and arched its way across the plain, graceful and peaceful.

"There," Papa said, and the whole lot of us stopped to follow his gesture to a hill cradled in a curve of the river. An octagonal tower stood at its crest. An outpost.

I glanced at my father. He didn't look surprised to see the fort, so he must have been heading for it specifically. He shaded his eyes with his hand and surveyed the tower.

From here, it looked mostly intact, if abandoned. Safe and defensible with the river guarding its back and only one way up the hill. There were no fields, but the land was arable. We'd be able to grow our own crops given enough time, and the legion's outposts were always stocked with supplies. Perhaps there was something left.

Papa stood for a beat longer, and I wondered how many years into the future he could see. I could imagine the next few weeks, full of hard work and hope. But could my father see further than that? Could he imagine a time in the future when we weren't worried about what to eat? Maybe he saw a settlement at the top of the hill, docks along the river, and fields stretching out into the plains.

"It's beautiful," Aunt Iulia said.

It really wasn't. But it was the first intact bit of civilization we'd seen in forever, and my family drank in the sight. Beside me, Max stood tall, and even though his arm was still in a sling from our fight at the villa, he wrapped his good arm around my shoulders and squeezed.

Maybe this was the end. I was so tired of walking and fighting and wondering.

Unfortunately, one thing stood in the way, and as we got closer, it became clear we wouldn't be able to get around it.

The River Lirein stretched between us and the hill, broad and deceptively lazy in the sunlight.

We stood on the bank, staring at a row of broken pylons jutting up from the water's edge. Clearly, a bridge had stood here, but it was long gone now. I shivered and clutched my elbows.

"What happened?" Claudia said, rubbing her nose. It was red and peeling after days in the sun.

Max got way too close to the water for my taste and touched the jagged edges of the support beams with his good hand. "Built with magic. It sheared right off when the Darkness came." He shook his head and stepped out of the shallow water back onto the bank. "Lazy."

I stiffened. Before the Darkness, magic wasn't considered lazy. It was the pinnacle of civilization. Why bother with anything else when you had perfection at your fingertips? Sewing clothes together with thread, starting fires with flint and steel were all considered novelties. Eccentricities used by street magicians to entertain the masses or small-time craftsmen to earn some money on the side.

Just because the world had changed, and the rules were different now, didn't mean we should mock the way we'd done things before.

But I'd been hoping to find a bridge and a mostly intact fort as well, so I couldn't really fault Max for his words.

Papa's eyes found my face. "They must have considered themselves safe from sabotage, this deep into the Empire," he said. "There's nothing wrong with that. But it means we'll need to find a way to cross."

I shuddered, unable to suppress the shivers that traveled down my limbs.

"I'm sorry," Papa said, stepping close.

He knew why I didn't want to get in the water. They all knew, now. I couldn't hide that bit of myself anymore.

Even Papa, who'd pulled me out of the Pit, hadn't guessed the extent of the damage. Not until we'd found a pond about three months outside Leu'aline. The air had been warm and the sun bright after the first long, hungry winter, and my competent, disciplined family had taken the chance to wade in and splash in the shallows like children. We'd washed out our uniforms and left them drying on the bushes.

But while they'd played and cavorted, I'd sat on the bank, arms wrapped around myself as if that would keep me from shaking apart.

Papa, in good spirits for the first time in months, had scooped me up and thrown me into the pond.

My screams had ended the fun that day.

"It's fine," I said, staring at the water gurgling past the supports. It was just water. It wasn't like it could drown a person or anything. "I'll be fine. We just have to get it over with and then we'll be fine." It didn't matter how many times I said it, I still wouldn't be able to convince myself.

But I wanted the fort to be our home as much as the others did.

Not too far from the remains of the bridge, we found a good spot to ford the river. Here, the Lirein was wide and shallow, only up to Max's waist.

Onc by one, they stepped out into the river carrying what little baggage we had over their heads.

I fought down a wave of nausea before stepping to the water where it lapped the bank. Ever since the Pit, even the sound of it was enough to raise goosebumps along my arms. The thought of being submerged made me want to crawl out of my skin.

Papa waded in front of me, holding his pack over his head with one hand as he coaxed me.

"I'm right here, just put one foot in front of the other. See how gentle it is? Just listen to my voice and keep walking. That's it, love."

I hated how I clung to the sound of his voice. But at least the others weren't standing around watching. Most of them were already climbing onto the opposite bank.

The water flowed slow and easy around my legs, but out in the middle, it grew swift and treacherous. Without meaning to, I started angling down the river instead of across it, subconsciously avoiding the deeper water.

"Aurelia," Papa said, his voice growing stronger as he realized I was getting farther away. He took one look at my face and said, "Stay there. I'll come to you. We'll cross together."

I would have done as he said. I would have planted my feet and waited to rely on his strength and steadiness, but pebbles shifted under the thickened sole of my left boot, and I swayed. Panic swept through me, and I flung myself backward to compensate.

I went down too fast to scream. Water closed over my head and the strength of the river swept my knees up and my head back so I couldn't find purchase.

Water in my nose, water in my ears, pressing in cold and fluid from all sides. It didn't matter that the sun burned overhead, I still felt like I was closed in a black box deep underground with my voice echoing against the walls.

My thoughts tumbled along with my body, and I wondered if you could drown in panic. One hand broke the surface, but all I grasped was empty air.

I was alone. Again. Maybe the last few months had been a dream, and I was waking up back in the Pit under all the water and the wreckage that wanted to kill me. Papa hadn't actually rescued me. I hadn't seen my brothers' faces or heard my mother's voice. I hadn't argued with Claudia or Decima.

I'd never see any of them again. Only the darkness. Only the black and the water.

Power slammed into me all at once as if I'd called it—maybe I had—and I reached with my hands and something else, something deeper, to grab the bank. With a heave that was more mental than physical, I hauled myself free from the river and shot through the air. I landed against the ground and rolled into a wet heap, gasping and spitting up buckets of water. I curled around myself and sobbed, tears running into the water streaming down my face.

"Aurelia!" Papa's voice. Breathless, higher than normal. Boots pounding against wet grass. "Aurelia." He fell to his knees beside me.

I tried to tell him I was all right, but I couldn't get the words out around my ragged sobs. Instead, I clung to the wet cloth of his breeches and pressed my face against his warmth.

He leaned over me, stroking my hair and shoulders, murmuring nonsense in my ears.

We moved on from the bank an hour later, after I'd steadied and stood and coughed the rest of the river out of my lungs. By then, I could appreciate with a desolate sort of humor that at least I'd managed to pull myself from the river on the correct side.

No one mentioned the fact that I'd used magic to save myself. I felt guilty enough as it was. Ashamed that I'd had to save myself. Ashamed that I'd used a piece of me that I'd promised to bury for them.

CHAPTER THREE

Those who came from the normal magi families were usually in and out of the Forge in a month or two. It didn't take long for them to make you think you were about to die.

I spent nine months and thirteen days there.

After the first eight, they were going to throw me out. One of the five or six failures. They told me I was too hardy. Too stoic. "You don't really believe you will die."

I suppose it was a kind of compliment. My mother and father raised tough children. But I was there for one thing, and by leaving I would be accepting that those eight months of suffering would have been for nothing.

So, I plopped myself on the floor and refused to leave until they tried again. One more, I told them. One more and if it doesn't work, I'll go.

I designed my own torment for that last attempt at Tempering. The Forgers insisted it would be harder, more effective if I didn't know what was coming, but I disagreed.

The hardest part for me was anticipating what came next. I put myself through every single thing I had hated about my time at the Forge, and when that was done, I went into the Pit.

A six-foot by six-foot hole at the bottom of the Forge filled with enough water you couldn't stand, locked with a trapdoor at the top of a wall too smooth to climb.

It was ironic how much I hated it, considering that my shortened leg didn't matter so much in the water. It was the great equalizer, treating me exactly the same as every other candidate.

Six days floating and treading water in the Pit and I decided the Forgers were right. I was too tough.

I'd go home, Papa would wrap me in his arms and tell me it was all right, but it wouldn't be. My family would never be more than brilliant strategists and soldiers, and I would be useless, talentless, magicless.

Except no one came to throw me out. I floated there in the silence and the dark, tears streaming down my temples into the water, and waited for the trapdoor to open. They would let me out soon. There was always a limit, a cut off when the Forgers said enough. The point was to make me think I was going to die, not to actually kill me.

They didn't come.

I cursed them with what little strength I had, my voice ringing from the walls. But of course, no one heard me. My voice gave out, and I fell silent, floating without thought, while hot and cold, pain and loathing roiled under my skin.

Eventually, I sank. There at the bottom of myself, I knew I would die, and it would mean nothing to anyone except a bunch of soldiers who were so determined and annoying and loud and so loved.

Something groaned above me, huge and malevolent, and I shot to the surface in surprise. The indistinct edges of my blackness buckled and twisted and the whole Pit heaved, water sloshing me into the walls hard enough to bruise.

It felt like the world collapsing around me and the tiny, selfish worry that I would never be a magi retreated from the greater panic that swamped me. I braced both hands against the warping wall and kicked out, keeping myself afloat as the darkness moaned like a dying beast.

By the time the world was still, my limbs trembled and I could only just keep my nose and lips above the water's surface. An ominous creaking came from above for hours afterward. But by then the din had settled into the back of my mind, constant enough to be ignored.

The heaving had reshaped the Pit, pulling a piece of wall out and down until it sloped into the water. I explored it carefully with shaking hands before dragging my exhausted body out of the water. I shivered in the air, but lying naked in the cold would still be better than floating for even a moment longer.

The trapdoor hung over my head, closer now. But even if I'd had the strength to stand, it would have been too far to reach. So I lay there, staring at it.

What had happened?

An earthquake? An explosion? It couldn't be an attack. Could it?

I swallowed, mouth suddenly dry even after days in the water. The Forge lay in the heart of the Empire, protected from accident and disaster by so many magi you couldn't spit without hitting one. If something was strong enough to affect the Forge, then it was strong enough to affect the entire Empire. And you could bet Papa and the others would be in the thick of it.

With a gasp, I rolled to my side and pushed myself up on my elbows.

Allfather's Pantheon, I had to find my family. I had to get out. I would not die here in the dark without knowing what had happened to them. Without seeing them again.

I scrabbled at the walls, not so smooth anymore but still sliding against my nails. I stood on my toes, reaching, fingers stretched as high as they would go.

Impossible.

I jumped for the trapdoor, and my legs, strained from days of floating and treading water, collapsed under me. The back of my head smacked the platform, and I lay there, spent and dizzy.

I should have tried again. At least once more, but my mind drifted, too taxed to do more than take one breath after another.

I would live. Even if it killed me, I would live.

I don't know how long I drifted in and out of sleep. When I look back on it, I'm still afraid to do the math and figure out how much of my life I spent in the blackness. Longer than I should have. But not as long as I could have. That's all I want to know.

Finally, more noise above woke me. But this wasn't the terrible grinding and groaning from before. This was voices, muffled through so much twisted metal. Several thumps and a clang and suddenly the trapdoor fell open, and I blinked *bleary eyes to focus on my father's face hanging above me, outlined by fuzzy gray light.*

I thought he was a dream, a hallucination, a vision given to me by the Allfather as I died at last, but when he lowered himself into the Pit to wedge himself on my platform, he was solid and warm and smelled of leather and oil and steel.

He wrapped me in warm blankets before he and my brothers raised me up out of the Pit into a world gone as dark and silent as my torment.

The fortress still stood, its eight walls thrusting into the sky. The legion was one of the few things the Empire had built from mundane means. So just as my family's uniforms were held together with thread and not magic, the bricks of the tower were held together with mortar.

Beside the tower hulked the barracks and the stables. Other forts around the Empire housed hundreds of troops and sported armories, blacksmiths, and cadres of magi. But this one seemed designed for one division. No more.

Papa had probably aimed us for one of the smallest forts he could remember for a reason. This place was more likely to be safe, deserted, and defensible by a small group like ours.

The deserted part looked true. No one stirred in the cleared ground around the tower, and the stables stood empty. Although, from the smears in the fire pit in the court-yard it looked like a lot of the stables' inhabitants might have been eaten.

Papa gave the hand signal to spread out and search.

Report back when done and call for help if anyone living was found. It was a familiar routine by now.

Even if I wasn't allowed to fight alongside them, I was still allowed to search. I moved carefully and quietly around the barracks with Claudia while Papa and the boys took the tower and Mamma and the others searched the stable. A cursory search revealed no sign of anyone living. Broken furniture and weapons lay scattered across the flagstones as if frozen at the end of a long fight.

But if there'd been a fight, the bodies were long gone. And I couldn't imagine an entire division just up and leaving without their weapons.

"Does this seem creepier than normal to you?" I asked Claudia as she poked through a pile of torn and burnt blankets.

"I'm not really sure what's normal anymore," she said.

I didn't have anything to say to that.

We moved out the door only to stop motionless on the threshold. The courtyard was no longer empty.

A man stood beside the greasy blackened fire pit, his hair long and unkempt, a patchy beard wandering over his chin. Mud and sweat streaked his bare chest.

He didn't really look any worse than other survivors we'd caught glimpses of so far. But there was a blankness in his eyes, a buried panic like there were things he was desperately trying not to think about, that looked too familiar to me.

The tattered pieces of cloth he'd tied around his waist with a cord were grimy, but in the afternoon light, you could still tell they'd been a royal purple shot through with gold like rays of the sun. The vestments of a priest of the Allfather.

Behind my shoulder, Claudia whistled a call to the others. The priest blinked at us but still didn't move.

Papa and the boys appeared from the tower first and the rest flowed into positions around the courtyard, neatly hemming the man in. He flinched when he realized we had him surrounded, but he didn't make any move to defend himself. Not that he could have. His arms and chest were thin with malnutrition and his hands shook as if he couldn't stop trembling.

"Hello," Papa said. He had the perfect tone of voice for meeting new people. That mix of firm understanding had served him well with his troops.

The priest's gaze locked on my father and then his uniform. Emotions flashed across his face, too fast to catch before his expression settled into blankness once more.

"Are you here to man the fort?" he said. "Is the Empire recovered enough to send replacements?"

Papa's gaze flickered to the rest of us who looked like nothing so much as a division of the legion. "No," he said simply. "The Empire is gone. There is no one left to give orders."

The man took this in without a change in his expression or posture. He stood as if the worst had already happened to him and the rest of the world couldn't possibly top it.

"I am Arch-General Namarus," Papa said, putting his fist to his chest. "This is my family. We have come from Leu'a-line in search of a safe place to settle."

The blankness in the priest's eyes slowly cleared as if my father's formal greeting reminded him of something. Maybe a better, more civilized time. It took him a minute, but finally, he raised a shaking hand and splayed his fingers across his bare chest in the manner of the Allfather Order.

"Cassian Marcellus. Second rank Keeper of the Allfather, assigned as Division Chaplain."

Papa gestured at the tower and barracks. "And where is your division?"

The priest, Cassian, turned on his heel and headed out of the gate and down the hill.

Was that his answer? Or a different sort of reaction?

Papa frowned and signaled the rest of us to continue our search of the fort before he followed the Keeper. But as Claudia moved back into the barracks, I stepped out into the courtyard and followed Papa and Keeper Cassian. There was something about the look in this stranger's eyes that repelled me and yet drew me forward. I didn't want to leave him alone with my father. But I couldn't tell if I was protecting Papa or the priest.

I limped through the gate, sore muscles complaining that I was demanding still more of them. Papa looked at me as I caught up, but he didn't send me back. I lifted the hem of my salvaged gown free of the mud and wondered if the division had left the fort to camp elsewhere.

I don't think Papa had expected such a long walk or he would have brought one of my siblings for back up. Here, around the other side of the hill, someone had built a crude bridge across this bend of the river. Papa glanced at me ruefully as we crossed the rickety thing, and I snorted at the absurdity of almost drowning less than a mile from a bridge. But eventually, the priest led us down a slope, and there carved into the side of a hill was a doorway, lined with uncut stone. I glanced at Papa, but Cassian walked straight down into the earth without a second look at us.

Papa drew his sword and followed carefully.

I swallowed. I liked small, dark spaces underground almost as much as I liked water. But my father was disappearing with a man I didn't know if I trusted.

I followed.

The narrow passage soon opened out onto a room dug out of the middle of the hill. Cassian lit an oiled torch with some flint.

Waist-high cairns built of stone and mud blocks crowded the space, looking like a crude city made up of little huts. Each cairn was marked with three lines of text scratched into the stone. Name, rank, and hometown? It was hard to read them in the dark.

But it was familiar enough I could guess they were graves, lined up with military precision. At least fifty of them. I looked at Keeper Cassian's mud streaked clothing with new understanding. Now that I was looking, I noticed his fingernails were torn and bloody, too.

"You built them a necropolis," Papa said.

Cassian looked around at his work with an expression I couldn't read. "It took me so long," he said. "But they deserved it."

"What happened to them?"

Cassian met my father's question without flinching. "I killed them."

CHAPTER FOUR

I don't know when I realized that the sun was black. I'd spent so long in the darkness of the Pit that the eerie twilight of the world above seemed like full daylight for too long. Delirium kept me from realizing the truth as my family nursed me back to health.

No one ever mentioned the way they found me. It was bad enough since Papa blamed himself for sending me to the Forge. But it would have been worse if they'd forced me to talk about it. Writing the words here is enough. At least for now.

It took weeks to regain the strength just to be able to do anything beyond sleep and eat. Thinking took more energy than it should have. But gradually my wits returned enough to learn what had happened while I'd been underground.

A couple of astronomers in an observatory in Leu'aline were the first to notice anything. A week before I went into the Pit, oblivious to the outside world, they noted a sliver of darkness moving across the sun. They warned the Council that an *eclipse was occurring, but no one thought much of it until the world was plunged into twilight. For three months.*

The black sun rose and the black sun set and our historians dug through the earliest records of the Empire to find stories of the Darkness that came before the birth of civilization. But by then, it was too late. It had been too late for centuries. Because the Darkness didn't just take the sun, it took the magic out of our world. Like water sucked through a straw. Magi couldn't draw energy for their workings anymore. The power flowing through the world's surface had disappeared entirely.

And slowly the things held together by magic began falling apart. Clothes and furniture were funny at first, but then buildings started to fall. Councilors started to die of sudden old age. Legionnaires in distant provinces were stranded as the portals they'd used for transport and communication collapsed.

The rumble I'd heard was the Forge collapsing. That great building with its columns and its glass towers reaching for the sky was now a pile of broken marble and shards.

If the Darkness had only taken the sun, the Empire would have survived. If the Darkness had only lasted a week, the Empire would have survived. But with no magic and no sun for nearly three months straight, the panic spread like a disease and those who had not been crushed under the weight of falling stone and glass began to prey on each other. Without magic, communication across the Empire froze, troop discipline fell apart, our government shattered without leadership, and an Empire that had stood for a thousand years fell to chaos.

I missed my father's birthday while I was in the Pit. But most of my family had gathered in our villa outside Leu'aline to celebrate. Either through sheer luck or a miracle of the Allfather, they were together when the Empire started to crumble.

Papa recognized the signs early and after only a week of the Darkness, he made plans to keep his family safe, regardless of what happened to the rest of the Empire. They left the villa before it collapsed, and he sent mundane messengers out to find the few family members who hadn't made it home. Max had been with his division, who'd treated the lack of orders like a holiday. Luckily they'd been posted close to Leu'aline, otherwise, he'd have been stranded like so many of our troops.

Not all of my family were as easy to find. We still have not heard from Aunt Priscilla's son, my cousin Lucius. Or Aunt Iulia's husband, Uncle Fas.

And I, of course, was the most inaccessible.

Papa led them all to the heart of Leu'aline, to the rubble of the Forge. I think he had planned to find documentation, something that told him where I'd been in the last days of the Empire. He didn't count on the level of destruction.

Despite everything, the Allfather must have been watching over me because Papa found one of the Forgers still alive, picking through the rubble. And with some persuasion from my father and brothers, that Forger happened to remember the one girl who'd gone into the Pit just before the Empire collapsed.

They dug. All eleven of them, with the Forger and his friends press-ganged into helping. Eventually, they found the trapdoor.

While I'd been underground, everything had changed. More even than I knew at the time.

For three months the Empire lived in perpetual Darkness without the magic it had run on. And by the time the sun came back—and with it, the magic—the damage had been done. The world would never be the same again.

That night, we slept between intact walls for the first time in months.

We'd spent the rest of the day clearing out the barracks while my father questioned Keeper Cassian. The priest refused to talk about what had happened to his division, but I don't think it was to keep the truth from us. He sat, staring at the walls as if our voices had filled his mind until it ran over, and all he had left to defend himself from the noise was frozen silence.

Papa wasn't satisfied yet, but he recognized trauma as well as any other commander, and thankfully, he left the priest in peace after his questions produced no response. Max, Valens, and Decima took turns watching him that night, but I didn't think we'd have any trouble from him.

I woke before dawn and climbed from my cot as quietly as I could so I didn't wake the rest of my family sleeping in the barracks. Stairs spiraled up the walls of the octagonal tower, and I climbed them to the roof, which afforded a clear view of the river and the lands surrounding us.

I paused on the top step when I realized the platform wasn't empty. Keeper Cassian stood at the edge, the low wall only coming to his knees. Decima sat on the opposite side of the tower, gray eyes trained on him, her unsheathed sword across her knees.

I squared my shoulders and stepped up onto the platform with a nod to my sister. She nodded back but didn't say anything when I settled myself beside the priest, looking out over the plains. She didn't even warn me to keep my distance.

We waited, silent and tense.

Eventually, far to the east, the sky grew gray and pink. A sliver of orange fire slid above the horizon, and I found myself holding my breath. Gradually the sun rose, a brilliant orb we had taken for granted for centuries.

I watched it as long as I could, my eyes burning and watering, until I finally had to look away.

The Keeper shivered so hard his elbow brushed mine and tears streamed down his face as he squinted. "I come up here every morning," he said. "Just to make sure it's still there."

My fingers curled around the edges of the blanket I had wrapped around my shoulders. "I know the feeling," I said. Murmurs below indicated the rest of my family had stepped outside the barracks to check the sun as well. I had a feeling every survivor across Térne did the same.

The scrape of leather on stone made me glance over my shoulder, and I caught Decima flowing to her feet. She gave me a significant nod, then deliberately sheathed her sword and started down the tower stairs.

I blinked. She didn't feel like she had to protect me from the priest? Or was this a tacit acknowledgment that I could handle him if he ended up being a real threat?

When I turned back, I caught Cassian watching her go.

"I know I am a stranger in a time when trust has run out," he said quietly, turning back to the view. "But I will not hurt you. None of you."

"All right," I said.

He tilted his head, forehead creased. "You trust me?"

"I've decided to, yes."

"Why?"

"You haven't done anything to earn my distrust."

He wrapped his arms around his filthy torso. "You haven't asked me about my division."

"No."

"Why?"

I opened my mouth to explain, then shut it again so I could think of the best words. It was a little too easy to remember the way my siblings' words had pounded against my ears after Papa had pulled me from the Pit. Each was beloved, but that didn't stop them from hurting.

"I think you've lived in silence for a long time. You'll talk when you're ready. I don't want to take that choice from you."

His eyes narrowed. I'd finally recognized the look he always carried with him. There weren't a lot of mirrors around anymore, but I imagined if I ever found one, I'd see the same look reflected back at me. It was the reason my family looked at me with such pity.

He stared for a long moment, unblinking. I let him, though the unwavering attention felt a little odd. Human decency said he should have responded, or at least looked away by now. But it was hard to judge human decency after the Darkness.

"You know," he finally said. "You know that silence can be its own kind of torture. And the absence of it is just as painful. But I'm wondering how you know silence so well. With a family like yours."

"The Darkness didn't leave anyone untouched."

"You feel it too, then. Like something in the world is out of place. Cracked. But you can't be sure if it's the world that's broken or if it's just you."

"Oh, I know it's me," I said with a desperate little laugh. "I think the world's putting itself back together. It's me that's having a hard time healing."

"Is that why they protect you?" He gestured down the steps to where we could hear my family starting their day. "They surround you. Even when there's only one present, they keep an eye on you."

My mouth stretched over my teeth but it didn't feel like a real smile. "They're keeping me safe from myself. I'm dangerous."

"Should I be afraid of you?"

Anyone else would have asked that with a smirk, taking in my slight frame, my mismatched legs, and my very unmilitary dress. Compared to the rest of my family I looked the most harmless.

But Cassian asked with a serious tilt of his head, his eyes going sharp for that one moment.

I stared hard at him, wondering about trust. Yesterday, in the necropolis he'd built, he'd handed us the utmost trust, labeling himself a murderer when we could have killed him on the spot. Could I hand him my trust?

My family knew my truth. They knew what I was, but I'd never had to tell them. They'd found out the same way I had. I'd never actually had to put words to it before or make the choice to reveal my truth.

I licked my lips, then put my palms together and gathered energy into myself. I poured it into the air cupped between my hands. Then I pulled them apart and ignited it with a whoosh.

The ball of fire didn't last long, it needed more to burn than just air, but the effect was impressive.

Cassian's brown eyes had gone wide and he stared at me. "Magi," he said, his voice a bare whisper.

It was weeks before I was well enough to travel. Constant submersion had left sores all over my skin, some of them angry and infected, and it took a long time for my body to get used to food again. But my family stayed there in the ruins of Leu'aline until I could walk with them. Max even glued together a new lift for my boot, since the old ones had fallen apart.

I think if it had just been Papa, he would have stayed in Leu'aline indefinitely, waiting for the Empire to crawl to its feet again or lifting it up on his own shoulders. But with all of his family to look after, he decided that we would seek safety and shelter outside of the city. It was too hard to scrape together enough to feed a family of twelve. And scavengers, looters, even cannibals roamed the rubble-filled streets sifting through the wreckage and the survivors for something to eat.

So, we left. And on the plains outside Leu'aline, we saw

the sun again for the first time. It came back as gradually as it had left, but those first few rays of unfiltered light changed the world for us again.

For me, it didn't just change the world. It changed my place in it.

I stopped noticing the change in the sun because, at the same time, magic poured back into Térne.

A blue-white light that had nothing to do with daylight blanketed the land, making my eyes water and sting. For the second time, my family waited patiently for me to recover, even without understanding what was wrong. Except I didn't recover. I could only get used to the constant wash of power and the gentle whisperings.

Before the Darkness, some of our time in the Forge was spent in classes that taught the basics of a magi's art. To streamline the process after our Tempering and to give neces-sary breaks from the ordeals of the Forge. So it didn't take me too long to guess what I was seeing.

This was vytl, the energy of the world. The energy a magi could call upon to create and manipulate magic.

At some point in my time in the Pit, I'd been Tempered. I'd gone in ordinary and come out a magi. But during the Darkness, without magic, I'd had no way of knowing.

Now, when at last I'd fulfilled the wishes of my family and become what they'd hoped to make me, I was more a liability than an asset.

After the Darkness, the survivors of the Empire fell into two different categories: those who just didn't trust magic anymore, and those who hated the magi who'd failed them.

With no court and no government, my family didn't need

the influence I'd won for them, they didn't need the magic I could provide for them, and they had to protect me from those who wished to eliminate all magi. As so many survivors did.

CHAPTER FIVE

Cassian stared at me, and I wondered which kind of survivor he was. Would he hate me for the magic I didn't know how to use properly? Or dismiss me as untrustworthy?

"Magi." His shoulders sagged a little. "You've been Tempered." He said it not like he was stating the obvious, but like he was realizing everything that meant. Most people knew what it took to Temper a magi. He'd be going through every story he'd ever heard about the Forge and what went on behind its walls.

"Yes." I tucked my hands under my blanket. The day would be warm but the air was still chilly this early.

"When?" he asked.

I laughed without mirth. "I don't know."

He glanced at me sidelong, one eyebrow raised, giving me a glimpse of a more civilized Cassian.

"It's silly, I know," I said. "I can't even be certain of something so important." I tipped my head back, letting the first rays of the sun warm my skin. "I was nine months into my trials when the Darkness fell. I spent days, maybe weeks underground in a pit of water until Papa and the others rescued me. It happened sometime in there. I didn't even realize it until magic came back into the world."

"I knew some magi. The ones posted with us. They never spoke of the Forge. Nine months," he said, considering it. "Nine months of pain and then...silence."

"The Darkness succeeded where the Forgers failed," I said. "And now my family can't stand to look at me. I went through hell for this." I held up my fingers and called a little flame to flicker through them. "And now I can't use it for all the guilt."

Cassian remained silent and still. He didn't fidget or feel the need to fill the air with apologies or false hope. He didn't tell me it would be all right.

And that was good. Because I didn't know if it would ever be all right again.

When I finally looked at him, he'd closed his eyes against the sunlight and his fingers clutched the frayed fabric at his waist. A Keeper of the Allfather was supposed to be dressed in layers and layers of intricate purple fabric shot through with gold. Every layer represented another god or goddess that had been adopted into the pantheon of the Empire. It was one of the things that made the Empire strong. When we conquered a new province, we didn't destroy the local gods, we allowed them in under the patronage of the Allfather. All worship was welcome.

His fingers convulsed and he let go of the fabric. "When the Darkness came," he said haltingly. "My division fell to chaos. There were no orders, no direction. The uncertainty brought out the best in some men and the worst in others. The good ones left, to find family or find help. The ones that stayed—" His voice broke.

I shifted closer. Not enough to touch him, but enough that he noticed.

He took a shuddering breath and straightened his shoulders. When he spoke, all traces of emotion had flattened. "The ones that stayed blamed the Allfather for abandoning us."

"And by extension, you," I said when he stopped speaking.

"I was his closest representative. They took their anger and their fear out on me."

"How long?" I said quietly.

"Three months," he said. "Three months until I couldn't tell which voice was the Allfather and which was my own pain. I thought if I could silence the pain, I would hear the Allfather again, so I hid. I assumed that without me they would stop."

"But they didn't."

"They went for the magi next. Blamed them for the magic leaving the world." His broken, dirty fingernails dug into the flesh of his arms. "They had no magic to defend themselves. But they tried anyway. They tried, and in a way, they succeeded. When I emerged, they were all dead. Every single one of them. The innocent along with the guilty."

He shivered, and I reached out, then let my hand drop before touching him.

"The next day the sun rose again."

"You did what you had to do."

"Did I?" he said like he really wasn't sure. "If I'd waited, even one more day...if I'd been strong enough to hold out, the sun would have risen and they would have stopped. They would have realized what they'd done and everyone else would be alive now."

"Or they might not have. They might have killed you."

"Instead, I killed them. I decided that my life was worth more than theirs. But it's not."

I wanted to say that it was. That felt like the right thing to say. But I think it would have been like him telling me it would be all right. It would be nice to hear, but it would be wrong.

"I listened to them dying, and I did nothing to save them. I hid from my own pain and they died because of it." Finally, he turned to me and I met his eyes for the first time since the sun rose. "I did not hide when your family came. And I did not hide what I did from you. I will not hide ever again. My life isn't worth protecting if it means I live in the dark and the silence while others die."

"Did the Allfather tell you that?" I asked. "Can you hear His voice again?"

The corner of his mouth lifted in a rueful smile. "No. I've lived in silence since that day."

Later that morning, my family gathered in the barracks to take stock of our situation. Only Valens was missing as he was guarding Cassian while we talked. Papa leaned against the edge of a table, the only one in the whole fort that remained intact, while the rest of us arranged ourselves on the floor and the straw mattresses.

"We have one important question to answer today," Papa said, crossing his arms and meeting each of our eyes in turn. "Do we stay?"

We all knew who would make the final decision on that, but Papa would never do so without consulting us. Even generals did not make decisions alone. They had subordinates, and scouts, and advisers. Also, younger officers they were trying to train.

"I guess that depends on what shape the fort is in," Max said.

Papa nodded and glanced at Claudia first. "What are the food stores like?"

She shook her head. "There isn't much. The division that was posted here made short work of everything that was preserved naturally, but there are seed stores that weren't touched and we have plenty of land we can start cultivating. According to the plans in the commander's office, there should have been a storeroom sealed up with magic somewhere, but that's out of our reach." She carefully didn't look at me.

Papa gave a nod that didn't reveal much of his thoughts and lifted his chin toward Max. "What about the fort itself?"

Max shrugged his broad shoulders. "Seems like it's held up well so far. But the walls will need regular maintenance if they're going to protect us. We have plenty of space. Maybe too much for a smaller group like ours to defend. I'd recommend we pull our forces back to the buildings themselves and concentrate on making them our last line of defense."

"A good chunk of the weapons were left out in the weather and aren't in great shape," Decima put in. "But there's still plenty in the armory to arm ourselves with."

"We'll never lack for fresh water," Mamma said. "And I doubt we'll find anywhere else that's as defensible. But I'm worried about the threat that's already within these walls. Should we even consider settling here if there's a murderous madman who calls this place his home?"

"He doesn't have to stay," Quintes said, exchanging a look with his twin.

I gaped at him. "Cassian was here first. Are you suggesting we kick him out?"

His mouth pulled down as he shrugged. "It was just a thought."

My teeth ground together. "To him, we're the invaders."

Mamma held out her hand, halting the fight before it began. "Exactly. We cannot take his home from him. But we also can't remain here without addressing the threat he poses."

"You can't just imprison him, either," I said, fingers clenched in my lap.

"Why not?" Max said.

"Do we have the right to do so?" I cast a beseeching look at my father. "What law would we be upholding? Ours? Or the Empire's? Because that's long gone."

Papa scratched his cheek. "It is. But are you saying murder should not be punished?"

"I'm saying confession is not conviction." My hand cut

through the air. "I'm saying, let's start out the way we mean to go on. And be sure of what we're doing. Are we going to continue the Empire's ideals? Or are we creating something new? Are we building the kind of home where one person makes a snap decision that changes everything about a man's life?"

Papa examined me for a long moment. "It's a good thought for the future. But right now, I'm trying to keep my family safe. That is my immediate goal."

"Mine, too," I said quietly, holding his gaze. "But civility must start somewhere. Even in the worst of the chaos, we were never the kind of family to just take without thought or judge without consequence."

Papa blinked slowly. "No. No, we were not. Nor do I wish to be." He straightened away from the table and clasped his hands behind his back, his gray eyes focusing inward even as he remained staring at me. Suddenly, I was looking at a general, not my father. "But if we're going to do this the right way, the man will have to tell his story."

"He did," I said, bowing my head.

"He spoke to you?" Max said. "How did you get him to talk?"

I cast a scathing glance at him. "I listened. I didn't assault him with words and questions he's lost the ability to deal with. I let him speak and I listened. You could try it sometime."

Max flushed, and Papa rubbed a hand across his mouth as if hiding a smile. "Are you willing to defend the Keeper?" he asked me. "I will hear your arguments."

I drew myself up and folded my hands so they didn't

shake. "I don't think he's a killer. We are far more vicious than he will ever be."

"He told us he killed those men," Papa said.

"Because he felt like he did. His actions might have resulted in the deaths of what was left of his division. But it was the men themselves who did the killing. They attacked their magi," I said shortly. "And their magi defended themselves. All Cassian did was try to escape his own pain."

"He hid?" Papa said, and I could see the judgment in his stiff shoulders.

"Yes."

"In a time of war?"

"Was it?" I countered. "Or was it a time of chaos? With no orders, and no chain of command. He was a priest. A non-combatant. He did what he had to do to protect himself. If you're going to condemn him for it, then you will have to condemn his entire division for the things they did during the Darkness. You will have to condemn everyone we ever meet for doing what they had to do in order to survive. Will you?"

He kept eye contact as he said, "No."

My shoulders drooped. "I don't think Cassian's harmless, either. But I'm more worried about the threat he poses to himself. He's been hurt. Our response should be to help him. Not imprison him."

"You sound like you understand him."

"I do." I understood him better than my family understood me. The loss, the sacrifice, the guilt wrapped up in who he was.

"Will he share his home with us? So that we may help him?" Papa asked.

I chewed my lip, remembering the way Cassian had stared blankly at my family, at the sun, at the world. "I don't think he cares one way or another right now. He's keeping the world at a distance. But I think it would be good for him to be around people again. People like us."

Papa was silent a long time before he finally spoke. "I trust you."

I took a bracing breath. It felt like the final verdict of a judge. But also like a father admitting his daughter might know something about pain. Pride and victory made my chest swell and my head rise. Was this what they all felt after a battle well fought?

He leaned back against the table again and gripped the edge. "We're staying then."

Aunt Iulia sobbed aloud and hugged her little boy while my brothers all clapped each other on the back. Mamma stood and joined my father to kiss him on the cheek.

He gave her a broad grin. "That means we'll need to work to make this place support us," he said, forestalling the rest of the celebration.

"We can start a garden immediately," Claudia said. "There are plenty of things to plant in the late summer and we can still yield a harvest before winter. But we'll need some tools. Hoes and rakes and things."

"We can scavenge from nearby houses," Quintes said. "There were one or two we saw on the way that would only be a day or two's trek from here."

"Look for some building supplies while you're out there, too," Max said. "To repair the walls. And we'll need a roof." He flicked his fingers toward the sky and the open barracks.

"I can look for the storeroom that was sealed by magic," I said, caught up in their enthusiasm. "If it survived the Darkness, there might be food or tools locked inside."

They froze, most of them glancing at Papa, and my heart leaped to my throat.

His lips thinned, and the lines deepened around the corners of his mouth. "That's all right, Aurelia," he said. "We'll see what we can come up with ourselves. No reason to rely on your magic."

It was the first time anyone had actually spoken the word out loud, and his voice went tight and strangled on it like he spoke of a shameful disease.

I flushed as that swell of pride and victory swept out of me, leaving me deflated. This thing I'd fought and suffered for, I couldn't use. Not even to help my family. Even talking about it made them wince. I was the extra once again. The liability. And the stark contrast to the confidence I'd felt while defending Cassian made me go cold all over.

None of them had ever treated me like spun glass before I went to the Forge. I'd been different from them, yes, but not fragile. This new hesitance had nothing to do with the way I walked and everything to do with the power hiding under my skin.

I bit my lip until the pain made my eyes water. I would not sit in the barracks twiddling my thumbs while the rest of them sweat and bled to make this fort our home. I would find something else to make me useful. Something that didn't involve magic.

CHAPTER SIX

I walked through the courtyard of the fort surveying my family hard at work.

Against one wall between the dilapidated stables and the barracks, Claudia bent to mark out a corner of the garden, hammering a stake into the soft ground with the back of her makeshift hoe. When we'd arrived, the entire courtyard had been paved, but after a couple of days of back-breaking work, we'd pulled the paving stones out of this section. After Decima had seen some distant figures moving around a far bend in the river, we'd decided to position our first garden within the walls.

Papa leaned over the edge of the well signaling Aunt Priscilla to haul on her rope. Between them, they might actually have the well cleared and usable by the next month. Thank the Allfather. I had blisters from carrying leaky buckets up the hill from the river.

I swerved to avoid the cloud of dust Mamma swept through the door of the barracks. Behind her, Aunt Iulia passed with a mop, made from a spear haft and a bundle of rags. I couldn't see her from here, but I knew Granmamma would be sitting inside somewhere winding new bowstrings for the weapons in the armory.

Everyone had a job. Everyone had something they were good at.

I ducked my head and opened my notebook to the page where I'd started a rough map of our buildings and the resources we'd tucked between them. My handwritten account of the Darkness was gradually giving way to notes on our present circumstances, musings on our attempts at survival, and lists. Stepping away from the barracks, I ran my finger down a column of numbers, trying to look industrious.

Maybe if I acted like I was good at something, I would start to feel like I was good at something. And the busier I was, the less I could think about that forbidden skill. At least with the notebook and a piece of charcoal in my hands, I felt mostly useful.

Max swore from atop the wall and paused to wipe the sweat from his brow. I added "fortify our defenses" to my list and bit my lip. Then I scratched it out and started a whole new page where I could organize the tasks under their own headings.

There was no way we'd ever have enough people or enough supplies all at the same time to get these things done. Not when it seemed like everything was a priority. Should we make Claudia take time out from planting to help get clean water through the well again? Or should we demand my brothers leave off hunting and scavenging to help Claudia, even if their hunting and scavenging was the only thing keeping us fed right now? And Max kept whining about the walls and how a concentrated force like the one we'd encountered at the villa could break through our defenses easily enough.

I chewed my lip and flipped back over my notes. Maybe in the winter when Claudia wasn't planting or harvesting and the snow kept us from scavenging very far, we could concentrate on the more urgent things that needed to be done around the fort. I tapped my teeth and made a note.

How bad would the snow be? The cities of the Empire had all been heated magically so only the barest snow would actually touch the ground. Just enough to be picturesque. Not enough to interfere with anyone's work. I made another note to ask Papa how the legion had dealt with weather out in the far provinces.

Movement caught my attention where Cassian lurked in the shadow of the open gates, his gaze darting from my father to Claudia and back to me. He still wore the remains of his robes tied around his waist, but at least he'd tried to wash his hands, leaving a stark line on his wrists marking where the grime started.

I hid a smile and shook my head. He was making an effort. That was what counted.

He didn't speak much, except to ask simple questions. And that was all right. I was careful not to touch him. Or push him into too much human contact right away. He could always retreat if he needed to. But I also made sure he knew where to find me. The rest of my family felt obliged to talk to him, a soothing incessant chatter. I knew they meant well, but I seemed to be the only one to appreciate the value of quiet.

In the last week, he'd spent more and more time following in my shadow, listening when we spoke, and I counted that as progress.

I paced the walls, checking on Max's progress, keeping half an eye on Cassian and the other half on my notebook. When I reached the other side of the well, raised voices made me look up.

"Can't you come down here for five seconds and help me with this? Food is more important than defense right now," Claudia called up to Max, who perched on top of the wall inspecting the mortar.

"And how do you think you're going to eat the food if you're dead?" Max shot back. "Get Quintes and Valens to help you."

"I haven't seen them today. Where are they?"

I flipped back a page. "They're out scavenging from that abandoned town to the east," I said, my finger on the list of things we needed but couldn't make. I'd copied it for them this morning. "They left early. But they should be back before nightfall."

Claudia rolled her eyes so hard her whole head moved. "That won't be enough time," she said. "I want to get some of these seeds in the ground today, but if I'm going to do that, then I need someone else to haul water from the river."

I shut the book with a snap. "What happens once you get them planted?"

Claudia gave me an incredulous look. "They grow." Then her face fell. "Hopefully."

It was my turn to roll my eyes. "I meant how much work

will it take then? If you get the seeds planted and watered today, will you have extra time tomorrow?"

She tilted her head, considering. "After I get everything watered and weeded? Yeah. I think so. I want to start another garden plot over on the other side, but I'll need everyone's help to clear more paving stones before that happens."

"All right, so Max, come down and haul water for Claudia now, so she can get her seeds planted. And tomorrow, she'll help you on the wall. We'll figure out a time when everyone can take a break from what they're doing to clear more ground for another plot. It might be a few days, but at least this one will be done, right?"

"Yeah, but—" Max started.

I lifted my chin to glare at him. The sun behind him made my eyes water but maybe that would make my expression fiercer. "Even if she dropped everything and came to help you, would you get the wall finished today?"

He hesitated. "No."

"Then this is a better use of time. And it still gets you back on the wall by tomorrow morning. And with two people you'll make more progress."

Claudia chuckled and held up the leaky buckets. "Hop to it, water boy."

I shook my head as Max grumbled his way down to the ground. "Don't gloat," I said. "You're just going to be carrying bricks and mortar tomorrow."

Her face fell, and I turned back to my book.

"This can work," I said. "We just need to break things down into manageable pieces and assign priorities based on need and time. Everyone is going to have to be a little flexible." I met both of their eyes again in turn. "Give me a list of everything you need to finish your projects, both supplies and manpower. We can't go forward on some things until we have the resources to complete them. But we might be able to get some prep work done. I'll draw up some work schedules. Shift rotations. And I'll keep lists of everything we need so Quintes and Valens know what to look for."

They both blinked, then grinned. "We'll be like a real division again," Max said.

"With Aurelia as dispatch."

I flushed. It wasn't something I'd ever thought I'd do. And it felt like the last job left over after everyone else was picked for something better. But it was important. And it was useful. I'd be helping, finally. And like Max said, I'd be a full member of the division.

It was a gradual change at first. So gradual none of us even knew it was happening. But as we made plans and saw their effects unfold, I could go back and see it all tracked in my notebook. Our focus shifted as we went from worrying about each day to worrying about the next month and the next year.

I could see it as we took down the temporary tarps over the barracks and replaced them with beams and thatch we'd cut ourselves from the grasses on the plains. I could see it as we bickered less about who was doing what and laughed more at our own expense. I could see it as Mamma hung curtains in the windows and my aunts made colorful quilts to decorate our beds.

It was such a small step to take, and it wasn't something I'd written in any of my lists. But it was the difference Papa had seen standing beside the river, looking up at the fort. The difference between surviving and thriving.

The leaves on the apple tree outside the gate had changed to a bright gold before Cassian allowed me to put my hand on his arm for the first time. Nearly a week later, he consented to even more than that.

I pressed his shoulders until he sat on the stool in front of me.

"Is this necessary?" he asked. It wasn't a facetious question. He really wanted to know. So long by himself, with only his thoughts and guilt to keep him company, had warped his memories of civilization.

"Humor me," I said and brought the comb to his hair, starting at the ends and working out the knots from the bottom up. The day before I'd coaxed him into a bath beside the hearth in the barracks. I'd had to trade a month of chores with my brothers to get them to haul the water from the river, but it had been worth it to see Cassian dip his hand into the tub over and over like a child learning the feel of it on his skin.

After I got most of the tangles out of his hair, I brought out a pair of scissors. I half expected him to protest, but he held still while I ruthlessly chopped off the excess and trimmed the strands around his face. In the end, the haircut looked a lot like Papa's, but my father was a handsome man so I didn't see anything wrong with that.

I trimmed up the straggling ends of Cassian's beard until I could actually run a razor over his chin. My brothers had made do with the edges of their swords for a long time, but Quintes had been collecting certain luxury items like soap and hairbrushes and razors from the surrounding area to use as bribes for his siblings.

I probably wasn't the best person to shave a man, but I didn't really trust the razor in Cassian's hands. We were probably past that danger, but why push it? Especially when this gave me the chance to normalize human contact a little more.

Under a year's worth of beard, he had a nice jaw, and who would have known there was a cleft in his chin. I stepped back and surveyed him. "You look very handsome."

He blinked. Then he opened his mouth and closed it as if searching for the right response. "Thank you," he finally managed.

That was a much better response than I'd expected. I wanted to squeeze his hand or give him a hug, but I didn't push it.

"Here," I said instead and handed him a bundle of clothes. The barracks wouldn't be empty for much longer. I'd only bartered for an hour of no interruptions from my brothers.

Cassian reached for the bundle, then stopped. "These are..."

Royal purple and gold gleamed at him from the pile. I licked my lips nervously before I spoke. "I found some of your old vestments and sewed them back together."

He frowned and tucked his hands under his armpits. "I can't wear these."

"Why?"

"You know why."

"Because you don't hear His voice anymore?"

A muscle jumped in his jaw, and he looked away. "I'm not worthy to be His priest anymore."

"Why?"

His eyes flashed in anger that was completely justified, and I hid a surge of satisfaction. "You know why," he said again.

"Because you hid." And because of everything that had come after.

His gaze flicked away.

I knelt beside him. "Cassian. You're not the same man who hid while others died."

He flinched, but I kept going.

"Just like I'm not the same girl who treaded water until she accepted death. I'll admit, I know very little about faith, and maybe you're right. Maybe that man shouldn't have been a priest."

His gaze came back to rest on my face.

"But maybe this one should." I put my hand on his.

He stayed silent, his thumb stroking the fabric of his vestments over and over.

"I'm not asking you to pray again," I said. "Or to hold services or preach. Just to wear the clothes."

I knew how well the clothes we wore shaped the image of ourselves. I'd taken one of the gold-tooled uniforms we'd found in the fort and made myself a sleeveless, leather cuirass to go over my dress. It looked a little ridiculous, but it made me feel like I had a place in my family without trying to be something I wasn't.

In the end, he took the vestments and disappeared into the tower to change.

I found myself humming as I swept up the discarded hair. Outside the barracks, I let the strands float away on the breeze toward the repaired stable where the new cow and a couple of chickens lazed in the sun. Valens and Quintes had found the livestock wandering the countryside without any obvious owners. And, of course, they were welcome to make their home with us. Their milk and eggs were even more welcome.

When I raised my head to take a breath, I noticed a group of people making their way up the hill from the river.

I stiffened, but Decima was already whistling the warning for unarmed visitors, and my family converged on the courtyard from their scattered chores.

By the time the group had reached the gate, Papa stood with Mamma beside the garden plot.

We relaxed when we recognized Valens and Quintes leading another man and a girl about my age through the open gates. Decima must have recognized them long before the rest of us, or they'd never have gotten this far.

Quintes stopped a few feet away and gestured to the man. He had a big bushy beard shot through with gray that was much better groomed than Cassian's had been.

"Papa," Quintes said. "This is Abele. He owns the farm about three miles west. He asked to speak with you."

The man glanced around our fortifications. "Are you the division commander?"

Papa's lips quirked in a grin. "I am the father. I no longer have a division to command."

Abele touched his fingers to his forehead. "Fair enough. My daughter, Cristina. We've come wondering if you are interested in trading."

Papa's eyes gleamed. "We are always interested in trade with our neighbors," he said as if we'd had any neighbors before.

Most of us had only been thinking of survival when Papa had led us here, a place where we could shelter from the chaos of the rest of the world. But of course, Papa had been thinking several steps into the future.

I wasn't the only one to glance at the garden where our crops grew against the wall. They seemed to be coming along nicely, but it was a slim bet that they'd be able to feed us through the entire winter.

I pulled out my notebook with all of its lists and stepped up to join Papa as Abele spread his arms wide. "We don't have much in the way of amenities, but my family has been farming this land for generations. And crops still grow without magic even if we can't water as many of them as we used to."

I flipped through my notes as they chatted, looking for my count of our eggs and milk. We also had plenty of weapons that we'd restored. Those might be a good trade if they had crops stored from a previous harvest. I should remind Papa to ask if they had a bull that could serve as a stud for our cow.

Papa and Abele laughed like old friends.

Until Cassian stepped out of the tower.

He'd combed his newly trimmed hair back, and the sun hit his robes, making the gold glint as the fabric swayed. I wasn't a skilled seamstress, so I hadn't managed to recreate the many layers and the way they shifted and moved to create patterns of starbursts, but they were still obviously the vestments of a Keeper of the Allfather.

He stood uncomfortably, blinking in the bright light at the newcomers.

Abele took a sharp breath and frowned. "You have a priest? Even after the Allfather abandoned us to the Darkness?"

Cassian's mouth tightened, and I wanted to smack the farmer. I'd only just gotten him back into his vestments, and that was only the first step to helping Cassian heal from everything that had been done to him. Now this man would ruin it all with just those words.

Cassian looked down, then he seemed to force his gaze back up to Papa. He raised his chin and stood. He didn't retreat or offer excuses. He could have said anything to deny his calling and profession, but he didn't. He just looked to Papa.

I glared at my father. Don't screw this up, I thought. Look at him. Look at him not hiding.

Papa studied Cassian, taking in his clothes, his stance, even his new grooming. Then he turned back, sparing a swift smile for me.

"He is a priest, yes. I will not take away his belief." Papa gestured at the newcomers. "The same way I will not take away your unbelief. Anyone is welcome here." It went unsaid that anyone who didn't agree wouldn't be welcome.

Abele blinked. With one sentence Papa had established our stance as a family and as a settlement. All they had to do was agree to a little tolerance.

It didn't take him long. He glanced back only once to meet his daughter's eyes. "Of course," he said. "Far be it from me to judge a man for what he has to believe to survive." He started following Papa again. "And at least he's not a magi. They're useless at best and dangerous at the worst."

The breath left my lungs, and I closed my eyes as Papa and Abele passed to draw up the first trade agreements for our new friendship.

CHAPTER SEVEN

Wind blew sheets of snow across the courtyard, but inside the barracks, we were at least moderately warm. A fire roared in the hearth we'd built at the southern end of the building and our new thatch roof only had minor leaks. Not bad for a lot of guesswork and Max's dubious memory. The stack of firewood would have to be replenished at least once a week throughout the winter, and I made a note of that on my list.

The others huddled close to the fire, resewing clothing we'd found in nearby ruins. Their chatter washed over me as I sat at the table running through the numbers in my head and my notebook. For once, my job was more important than theirs. This math could save our lives.

I tapped my teeth with the end of my pencil—Max had made it for me a couple of months before and it had made my writing much more legible. I added another number to the column. In the fall, we'd found another unclaimed cow, but then we'd lost one of the chickens to disease before we'd even known she was sick.

But with the six or seven pails of milk we got a day and the eggs from the remaining chickens, we actually had a good buffer going. I even knew exactly how many potatoes and ears of corn were stored in the cellar.

We could still trade with Abele and his family, but the three-mile walk was an arduous journey in this snow, so we couldn't count on them all the time.

Still, as long as nothing drastic happened I was pretty sure we could make it through the winter without starving.

It was an odd feeling to sit here and calculate how long before we all died, but considering I'd already almost starved to death once in my life, seeing the numbers laid out like this was strangely comforting. We could make it work. We'd all be a lot leaner come spring, but if we could still hunt and fish through the snow, we could survive.

A burst of laughter rang out, and I glanced over to see my brothers grinning and Cassian blushing in the flickering firelight. He kept his head ducked as he sewed. The Keeper wasn't as easy with the rest of my family as he was with me but at least he was sitting there, speaking when spoken to, working with the rest of them. My brothers included him in their jokes and Mamma always asked if he was cold, would he like another blanket? Like he was part of the family.

A clatter and a raised voice made me jerk, and Papa and Claudia each glanced up. The rest of them froze as we strained to hear over the wind.

There was another voice that definitely didn't belong to

Decima, who stood watch on the walls tonight. Had someone breached our defenses in the storm?

Papa moved to the door, collecting his weapons and shrugging into his leather cuirass before throwing open the door. The rest swarmed to their feet, catching up swords and bows, moving swiftly and confidently.

I tossed down my pencil and took up my own bow before following them out into the snow.

The cold hit me like a wall, and I sucked in a breath but kept moving. Nothing lit the courtyard except the streams and flashes of vytl that only I could see, but we knew our home well enough by now. My family spread out before a shout brought us to the door of the stable.

"There!" Papa called.

Several figures slouched beside the door as if to force it open, and my brothers shouted for them to stop where they were. Voices rang around the courtyard and there was the shing of metal as Decima unsheathed her sword and leaped from the wall behind the stable.

I drew my bow and trained an arrow on the group of invaders, squinting through the swirling snow.

Two men and one woman stood around a cluster of children, darting glances between all of us. One of the men held his hands up, but the other grabbed for the hilt of a rusty sword swinging from his hip.

Not a good move around a family of soldiers. Max and Quintes surged forward and my fingers tightened on my bowstring.

The woman's eyes widened, and suddenly the flits and

flashes of vytl around us snapped into lines, racing for her. She raised her hands and the power poured into her.

My heart leaped to my throat. Magi. She was magi and she was about to attack my family.

I dropped my bow and yanked the lines of vytl back toward me, gathering the magic in my hands. I didn't even know what I was going to do with it except blast anything that looked like a threat.

But instead of attacking, the magi flung out her arms and gathered the children to her, her power washing over them.

A shield. She was shielding them. From us. We were what they were afraid of.

A wave of cold that had nothing to do with the snow swept through me, raising the hair on my arms, and I dropped the vytl I'd collected. It washed over my skin, unchecked, burning as it went. But I stifled my cry of pain. Allfather's Pantheon, what had I almost done? What would have happened if I hadn't hesitated?

Papa reacted a split second later, seeing only three frightened adults trying to defend a group of children. There was no mighty enemy here.

He shouted out in his parade-ground voice, "Hold your fire."

I'd already abandoned my bow, but Granmamma and Aunt Priscilla pointed their arrows to the ground, strings relaxed. Decima halted her headlong charge by catching herself against the corner of the stable. The rest of my family fell into parade rest, keeping their weapons close, but down and non-threatening.

"Who are you?" Papa stepped forward so it was clear he was in charge. "What are you doing here?"

The man who'd held up his hands gulped, his throat bobbing. "We didn't mean any harm. We were looking for someplace warm. The children..." He trailed off as he glanced behind him. The children, who'd been shivering moments ago, had stopped. That couldn't be a good sign.

Papa's sharp eyes took them in, narrowing on the children wrapped in threadbare blankets. He signaled Max and Quintes.

"Go with Decima to secure the perimeter. Figure out where our breach is." He met my mother's gaze. "Gather some more blankets and tell Claudia to find some more bowls."

He turned back to the intruders and snapped his fingers. "The rest of you. Inside. We can sort this out in the barracks at least."

"We were just looking for shelter," one of the men said after they'd been herded inside.

Mamma and Claudia were busy drying the children off in front of the fire, while the rest of us faded into the background a bit so we didn't look so threatening.

The man pushed wet black hair out of his eyes and glanced anxiously around the barracks. "We needed a place to wait out the winter. We didn't see any lights or—or people in the storm. By the time we realized there were animals in the stable, it was too late to ask permission. We thought maybe you wouldn't notice us for just one night and we could slip out in the morning."

Papa blew out his breath. A couple of the children were crying now as their limbs thawed out, silent tears streaming down their cheeks.

"Have you been caring for your siblings since the Darkness?" Papa said, rubbing the back of his neck, a sure sign he was thinking.

"W-we're not related," the man said, indicating the other two adults. "Not really. We just sort of found each other and we couldn't leave the kids to fend for themselves. They didn't have anyone else. We've tried to settle a couple of different times, but no one wants to take in children who can't work for their keep."

A muscle in Papa's jaw jumped, a sure sign he was clenching his teeth. He glanced at me, and I knew what that expression meant. Could we help them? Could they stay? It might have been his decision ultimately, but I was the one with the math.

I ran the numbers in my head, adding six more mouths to the equation. I'd pored over them enough in the last day or two to have them memorized.

"It'll be tight," I told him quietly. "But if we're all willing to sacrifice a little—and we don't lose anymore animals prematurely—we can make it work."

The smile he gave me lit up the room, and he turned to give the group the good news.

The newcomers might have written this off as a passing kindness, but I recognized the gleam in my father's eye. He was looking into the future even as Mamma wrapped them in spare clothes and Claudia handed around bowls of soup.

How long did it take to adopt someone? Days? Weeks? It seemed my father could look at someone and decide to protect them in only a matter of moments.

It wasn't that far out of the way. We'd already done it with Cassian. He was as much a part of our family now as any of us.

We weren't just building a home for the Namarus family. We were building a home for anyone who needed one.

I spent the rest of that night passing between the newcomers, asking them questions about their history, writing down everything I could, making lists of their skills. In the morning, I'd start over on the duty roster, fitting them into our routine.

I left the magi for last. She glanced up at me, twining a strand of hair around and around her finger as I settled myself on the floor beside her. A dark curl fell over one brown eye. She didn't look any older than Max at twenty-five, but that was old enough that she had definitely been a magi before the Darkness.

"I'm Aurelia," I said.

"Helena," she responded, voice hushed.

I found a blank page while she watched.

"What are you writing?" she said.

"I've been the one to organize our schedules," I said. "I make sure everything gets done when it has to be so that we have time to help each other out on all the projects. It's a little easier in the winter now that we don't have planting and watering."

She nodded, eyes still on me.

"Do you have any special skills?" I said. "Anything that would help us?"

"I can write and do figuring," she said quickly as if we'd kick her out if she didn't come up with something useful. "And Antony taught me how to skin and dress game. Oh, and I can sing." She blushed. "If that matters at all."

I chuckled. "None of us could carry a tune if it provided a handle so you'll be welcome on long winter nights." I paused, pencil poised over the page. "Is there anything else?" I made sure to keep my voice quiet so only we could hear.

She went white, then flushed again and shook her head. "I was a soldier, but not...not like that." She made a quick sharp gesture to my brothers in their uniforms. "You saw what I can do, but I try not to use it anymore. It's not worth it."

I ran my thumb over the tip of my pencil. "Do they know?" My gaze flicked to the two young men she'd been traveling with.

She shook her head. "No. No one wants...us around. Not anymore. Is it different here?" She glanced around at my family and accidentally caught Max's eye. He grinned at her.

I opened my mouth to answer but found I didn't really know what to say. My family didn't hate magi, but the way they avoided the subject, like magic had never existed in the first place, was almost worse.

Helena saw my hesitation but not the reason behind it, and she reached forward to grip my fingers. "Don't tell anyone. Please? I've managed to keep it from them so far and I can live without it. I really can. Magic isn't worth it if it causes so much damage."

Caught up in her fear, I covered her fingers with my hand. "I won't. Don't worry, I won't tell. And you don't have to be afraid anymore. You're safe here."

CHAPTER EIGHT

Looking at the ruins of our cities or out across the empty plains in the center of the Empire, you'd think there were no more survivors. That they were all dead or scattered.

But so many still needed a home. So many still needed family and friends. They needed the chance to make that choice between surviving and thriving.

The fort offered shelter. And those who gathered there offered the rest.

They trickled in from all over the Empire, refugees of the collapse still searching for a reflection of what they'd lost. And we made our home their home and our family their family. Because we needed to thrive, too.

I picked my way through the crowded courtyard avoiding a group of children playing with a gray dog that had somehow found a home within our walls. They squealed as they chased the dog and the dog chased the ball, all of them watched over by Aunt Iulia.

I slid a finger under the leather edge of my cuirass which had grown hot in the summer sun. Sweat trickled down my ribs but I didn't want to take it off for the sake of a cool breeze. It marked me as part of the Namarus family and with so many settlers in the fort now, we needed to be noticeable. In case anyone needed to find us quickly.

Helena paused beside me to take in the rough frames of the house Max was working on. This one stood right up against the wall with no space in between. Our population had doubled over the previous winter and spring. And while the barracks had originally been built to house a division, Papa had started on plans to build some single-family homes just inside the walls.

"I can see them starting to pair off soon," he'd told me privately. "Disaster brings people together and now that we trust each other, there will be families, children, new life. It's inevitable." The words made it seem like an inconvenience, but he'd smiled when he'd said it and I could imagine he was hoping for some grandbabies of his own.

Beside me, Helena stared at my brother, who worked shirtless on top of the wall. He bent to lift a corner of the roof into place and caught her gaze. I rolled my eyes when he flexed just for her.

Given the way Max had been making eyes at my new assistant, he was probably just waiting for one of these homes to be done before he made it official.

Marriage. What would that look like in this new world we were building? Without a government, what would keep two people tied together except their own determination and commitment? Maybe that was better than anything the empire could have contrived anyway.

I nudged Helena in the ribs, and she flushed when she realized I'd caught her staring.

"Sorry," she said. "Where were we?"

I handed her the slate Quintes had found for me and the white stone that served as well as chalk and gave her another nudge. "Why don't you go ask him if the builders have anything to add to their list."

She bit her lip and ducked her head, but she took the slate and wound through the messy construction to speak to Max.

Helena had been my unofficial assistant for months. With so much to keep track of now, I should probably promote her. I still knew everyone's name; I knew all their faces. I spoke with them every day. But it was much harder to organize schedules when there were over thirty people and several family groups that all had opinions and different ideas about what was a priority.

Especially since it changed day by day. Every time one thing got crossed off the list, something else rose up to replace it. Clean water hadn't been an issue in months, but now we had to worry about privies and designated clean zones. My favorite job so far involved telling a bunch of refugees who'd just survived winter on their own that they couldn't poop just anywhere.

I rubbed my lips to get rid of an inappropriate snort and gave Helena a smile as she came back. Something caught her eye over my shoulder, and I turned to look.

At the top of the octagonal tower, Cassian stood in his Keeper robes, light glinting from the gold.

He climbed the steps every morning as the sun rose. The first few months, I'd climbed with him and stood silent as he struggled without speaking.

Even now, he just stood there alone with his face turned to the sun as if that was all he could manage. No one bothered him. No one protested what he was doing. But no one joined him either.

I sighed and started back around the courtyard, but Helena caught my arm.

"Wait," she said. "Look."

I glanced back up. Another woman, older with her hair covered by a ragged scarf stepped up beside Cassian. They spoke for a brief moment. Then they both turned to face the sun together.

My hand crept to cover my heart which ached fiercely, and I blinked to clear the mist from my eyes. It was good. I couldn't tell if they prayed together or not, but whatever it was, seeing Cassian welcome someone else into his space was good.

Helena and I moved through the chaos, past more homes that stood half-finished, waiting for scrap from surrounding ruins. An old man gestured with gnarled fingers. One of the few survivors from the Empire who knew how to carve things out of wood and stone, who'd been considered eccentric because he'd worked with his hands, not magic.

He was one of our greatest resources. But he was only one man and we had so much to do.

We left him behind as he showed a young man how to

drive a nail straight and passed through the gates. Decima waved from the wall, a small squad of recruits arranged around her, clutching their weapons tight as they surveyed the horizon. Bandits rarely attacked the fort itself. We were too big and presented too much of a risk, but they did try to pick our people off as they returned from scavenging and hunting.

Beyond the gates, several figures toiled in the two fields we'd managed to clear and plow in the spring, and I deliberately made for the group working the line of corn nearest the fort. A middle-aged man with a bald head shining in the sun led them down the rows, weeding and watering.

"Renallius," I said to catch his attention.

He shouted a greeting, gave his workers a quick instruction, and then bounded over. He ran a dirty hand over his head, leaving streaks of dirt smeared across his scalp. "Aurelia," he said, voice pitched as though he spoke to a crowd. "How are you this fine day? How's the family? You holding the fort?"

"Always," I said. "Is there anything you need? Are the new ones working out for you?"

"Oh, of course, of course. Anytime we get someone new, they're willing to do just about anything just so they can stay."

I gave him a playfully suspicious look. "You're not abusing your power among all these impressionable youth, are you?"

He scoffed as I took careful stock of his workers and their needs. They all wore grins as he bounced back over to oversee their progress.

I shook my head. Renallius made everyone smile.

You'd never know he was magi.

We had a few of them now. I'd gotten really good at spotting them as they came in. They were the ones that were too quiet, who barely opened their mouths or drew attention to themselves. Or they were the ones who were too loud, talking about anything and everything other than magic. They were the ones with the sad eyes and the tight desperate smiles like they'd lost something important once and didn't trust it now that it was back.

They lived among the others, pretending they were like everyone else.

I usually spotted one sneaking in with a new group, hiding in plain sight. And I always made an effort to find them, to make sure they knew they were welcome. To talk to them. But not about magic. Never about magic.

A new one had come in just this week. He stood at the edge of the river watching Mamma and some of the others bringing in the day's catch. His tongue darted over his parted lips, and I could imagine him sizing up all the meals this one day's worth of work would make. The new ones were like that. Not just magi. Calculating days of hunger against a brighter future.

I stopped beside him while Helena lingered nearby with the slate.

He glanced at me out of the corner of his eye, his gaze taking in my dress and the cuirass over top. Even after only a day or two in the settlement, he probably didn't miss the significance.

"Hello," I said. "I'm Aurelia."

"Titus," he said. He tried to give me his full attention but his gaze flicked and I realized he was distracted by the flow of power around us. I could see him tracking a line of vytl. He hadn't learned how to ignore it yet, I guess.

"Welcome, Titus. I'm just here to ask you some questions if that's all right."

"Sure."

"How did you come to be here? Did someone send you, or did you find us on your own?"

He shrugged, his dark hair swinging across his shoulders. He brushed it out of the way. "I've been on my own for a while. I saw the fort and some of your hunting parties and I thought 'hey, I could do with some company,' so I came. Figured you could use the extra help."

I blinked. "That's...usually true. How did you survive the Darkness?" A casual question in this day and age, but it told us a lot about a person and what they were like when all the light of civilization left. We were perfectly willing to give broken people a second chance, but Papa wasn't in the habit of sheltering anyone who wanted to murder us in our sleep.

"My family," he said. "They made sure we had enough to eat and stayed out of the cities where all the killing went on. My father was a farmer."

I raised my eyebrows. "Really. That would be useful around here. We have a couple of areas where you can help out for now. Then, when we've gotten to know you a little better, we can move you to something a little more fitting and permanent."

I didn't tell him that we'd be watching closely to see how

he fit in with the settlers first. Mistrust wasn't a rule here, but caution was.

He bounced on his toes. "All right."

"Claudia and Renallius would love your help in the fields. We have a few more mouths to feed—"

"Nah," he said, interrupting me. "I did enough of that at home."

"Oh, well..." I stumbled. Most of our newcomers were so grateful for a home that they jumped in wherever they could. But I wasn't going to fault Titus for having an opinion. "Do you have any medical knowledge? We haven't found a healer for the settlement yet."

He shook his head so his hair flopped. "Not unless it's cows and stuff, but I'm done walking through the muck."

My jaw started to ache and I realized I was clenching my teeth. I forced myself to relax. Just because Titus didn't fit the mold of our more traumatized citizens did not mean I could kick him out on his rear.

"We could always use more people with the hunting and scavenging parties," Helena put in. "Especially now that we have to go farther and—"

"Can't I do something with magic?" he said.

I froze and shot a look at Helena. She stood with her mouth hanging open.

None of the magi had asked that yet. None of them had wanted to use their magic at all and definitely not publicly. Every single one of them had lived through the Darkness when they couldn't trust their own power, and then they'd lived through the aftermath when no one else trusted *them*.

Could this kid have managed to escape all that? Could the Darkness and distrust have left him unscathed?

"When were you Tempered?" I asked gently.

"What's that mean?"

I sucked in a breath. How...how could he not know what that meant? Every magi had been to the Forge. Every single one.

"The Forge," I said again, slowly. "When were you at the Forge? When did you become a magi?"

"Oh, the Forge," he said, face lighting up. "That was that old school for magi, right? I figured that was gone like the rest of the cities. I never went there. I started seeing the lights and being able to use them a few months ago when my family died." He held out his hands, staring at them intently and I realized he was about to summon up some sort of working.

I reached out and pushed his hands down. "It's called vytl and we can teach you how to stay in control. So, you became a magi recently. Since the Darkness."

"Yes." He rolled his eyes like I was being slow and in that moment I felt positively ancient. "I want to use it. What about there?" He pointed to the wall where the top of some scaffolding was just visible. "I want to build something amazing. Like the old magi." He flung out his hands, and I fought the urge to grab them again. Would I have been this arrogant if there had been no Darkness and I'd never learned to fear my power?

I took a deep breath and exchanged a worried look with Helena. This wasn't a conflict I thought I would ever have to deal with. Everyone knew magic wasn't dependable. Not like wood and stone and mortar.

"We don't build with magic," I told him, holding his gaze seriously. He'd have to learn sooner or later. "We want to avoid the mistakes of the Empire. We want to build something that lasts. And if it's going to last, it can't depend on magic."

He reared back, brow furrowed. "Is that some kind of law?" he said. "Did that general guy say we're not allowed to do magic?"

My fingers curled around my slate, and I forced them to relax. "No," I said firmly. "The Arch-general hasn't made any rules against the use of magic. But it's an unspoken agreement between the magi of this settlement and the rest of the people here."

He tossed his head. "Unspoken? So they're all just afraid."

"Yes, we're afraid," I said and held out my hand, letting a brief flame flicker across my palm. The light caught and reflected in his wide eyes until I snuffed it out. "We don't talk about magic. We try to forget about it."

He snorted. "That's stupid. Magic is still here whether people like it or not."

I opened my mouth, but I didn't know how to respond. I sort of agreed with him. Magic was still here, even after the Darkness had tried to take it away. Ignoring it wouldn't solve the problem. But rubbing it in everyone's face would only make it worse.

"It's all the magi here," Helena said, quietly. "If you start something, it's not just yourself that you're risking. You'd be putting every magi here in danger. We've all made our decision to not draw attention, to keep things under control.

Maybe one day things will be different. But the memory of the Darkness is still too close to the surface. Too many people remember what it was like when magic failed and the cities fell."

"It would be very selfish right now to expose an entire group of people just because you want to do something more exciting than farming," I said, trying to be delicate.

He frowned and scuffed at the dirt with his toe, obviously not happy with it all. I didn't want him to feel unsafe in the fort. We hadn't had a problem with anyone abusing or assaulting magi. But I wanted him to understand how serious the situation was and the type of power he wielded. The reason we hadn't had a problem was because we had kept the magi out of sight and out of mind.

"I know it's not very fair," I said, feeling like I was talking to my five-year-old cousin. "But these are the rules you'll have to agree to if you're going to stay here. At least for now."

"Fine," he said. "Put me down for hunting. At least it's better than digging in the dirt."

CHAPTER NINE

The weather cooperated for the first official wedding at the fort. The sun shone off the two inches of snow and sparkled through the icicles that hung from the eaves. I stood beside Helena while she held my brother's hands on the steps of the fort. We hadn't found any silks or jewelry like the brides in Leu'aline, but she looked immaculate in her blue linen gown with a new leather belt around her waist. And she'd carried a bouquet of carefully dried summer flowers. Her curling brown hair fell in masses around her shoulders, but Max's eyes never left her face.

Max had agonized over his outfit every bit as much as Helena had, but he'd finally decided against the legionnaire's uniform and settled for a simple tunic of soft green over his linen shirt and breeches.

"We're starting something new, here," he'd told Papa. "I don't want to get it confused with the old."

Cassian folded his hands in front of him, but I was the only one close enough who noticed the way he trembled.

When he spoke, his voice carried across the entire settlement crowded into the courtyard.

"Do you promise to love, honor, and respect each other?" he said.

"Yes," the couple said in unison.

"Do you promise to always hold the other as first in your life?"

"Yes," they said.

"Then may you be forever bound in love and life, through hardship and harmony. So say I."

"So say we all," the crowd shouted and cheers rang out against the walls.

Short and simple, just the way they'd wanted it. And Cassian had definitely cut out all the stuff about "my property will be your property and my titles will be your titles." Property didn't mean the same thing anymore. And without an official government, granting your spouse all of your rights as a citizen was pretty pointless.

Through all the noise, Helena and Max beamed at each other. I nudged Helena in the back at the same time Claudia bumped Max and the two finally threw their arms around each other. Another cheer went up.

A boom and a crackle made me jump and duck. Light streaked overhead and gathered in a ball only to burst into a cascade of sparks, falling over the crowd.

I caught my breath. Fireworks. The effect was beautiful but nothing in the natural world produced fire without fuel. Only magic. I straightened and cast my gaze out over the crowd.

The effect was obviously supposed to be festive, but

murmurs swept through the gathered settlers as they cowered and pointed toward the sky. The healer clutched her daughter's arm and the blacksmith scowled at his neighbors.

I exchanged a glance with Decima, who moved away from the wedding party to weave through the crowd. She touched two or three of her guard recruits and beckoned them with her.

"Magi." I heard the whisper start from the back of the gathering and move forward. "Magi in the fort. There are magi here."

My fingers clenched around the stems of Helena's bouquet. There'd been magi here since the beginning, but so many people still didn't know that. And I knew exactly who to blame for this little display of power. My eyes scanned the crowd, but I didn't see him. Maybe he'd realized what he'd done and run.

Beside me, my father clapped his hands, making me jump. "My friends, it's time to celebrate. I don't know about you, but I'm planning to store up for the rest of the winter." He patted his still lean belly which got him a laugh and he led the way through the gates to the rough tables we'd set up on the hill outside the fort.

I blew out my breath. Trust Papa to calm the crowd.

Although the damage was already done. There were still uneasy looks passing through the people below, and there would be no escaping the rumors now.

Helena took my arm. "Do you know who that was?" she asked in my ear.

I nodded. "It had to be Titus."

Her grip tightened, but Max joined us before she could say any more.

"Don't worry," he said. "Even magi can't ruin today." He kissed her temple before Quintes dragged him away with a joke.

"You still haven't told him?" I asked under my breath.

She bit her lip and wouldn't meet my eyes. "No. It doesn't matter. It's not a part of who I am anymore."

I frowned, but it was Helena's decision. I couldn't make it for her. That was why I was so angry with Titus.

"Go on," I told her. "Enjoy your feast. I'll deal with this."

I made my way down the steps and across the slushy ground, trampled by a hundred feet. People still milled in little groups, and I was stopped three times before I got to the gate. Anxious magi gripped my arm, voices tumbling over and over in my ears.

"Who would risk everyone?" they said.

"Will we have to leave? Will we have to fight?"

"What are you going to tell your father?"

"Will you take care of it, Aurelia?"

"No one will have to leave," I told them, patting hands, gripping shoulders, moving with purpose, and projecting a calm I didn't quite feel. "No one is fighting anyone. No one will be allowed to hurt you. We welcomed everyone here and we meant it, all right? Go enjoy the feast. I hear there's cake. I'll take care of it."

At the gate, I took a moment to stop and stare at the strands of vytl flowing around me. I didn't have to gather any of them up to find him. I could see his trail through the eddies and swirls of power, and I followed it.

Titus stood behind the stable, glancing around the corner at the crowd with the smuggest grin on his face.

"Titus," I said quietly.

He jumped and put his hand to his chest, but his grin returned less than a second later. "How did you find me?"

I frowned. Did he think I was stupid? "What did you think you were doing?" I said, planting my hands on my hips.

His shoulders hunched. "It was just supposed to be something nice for Helena and Max," he said. "Not anything serious. Why is everyone so upset?"

"How do you not understand what you've done? This is a much bigger deal than just some light in the sky. You've made everyone realize there are magi in the fort. You've forced the rest of us out into the open."

"Well, maybe I'm tired of hiding," he said, glaring at the dirty flagstones under his feet. "Magi are powerful. We can help everyone. We can be way more than farmers and hunters and, I don't know, stable boys. Why are we cowering in the shadows, letting everyone else tell us what we can and can't do?"

I forced myself to breathe even while my hands curled into fists. "Do you remember the fall at all? I know you don't remember climbing around in the ruined cities, searching for food, searching for dead loved ones. But maybe you can imagine it at least. Buildings collapsed with people still inside. Families were separated, scattered miles and miles away with no way to find each other. People died. All because magic failed. Do you really want to go through that again? Do you really want to put the world through that again?"

He scoffed. "The Darkness won't happen again. That was a one-time thing."

"Not true." I threw my hands in the air. "There was a Darkness that came before the Empire was ever established. This was the second. There could be a third."

He gaped. "I didn't know that." He sounded like it was some great unfairness that he didn't know everything.

I crossed my arms over my chest just to keep them anchored so I didn't throttle him. "You can't make decisions for everyone based just on how you feel. You've forced everyone out into the open, all because you wanted to feel special."

I regretted my words as soon as I had uttered them, but they were true. I'd wanted to throw his selfishness in his face since the day he'd arrived, but that wasn't the way to convince him.

And from the way his face went white, then red, and he spun away to storm through the gates, I'd just made things worse.

I rubbed my face.

"Is he going to be a problem?" Papa asked from behind me.

I didn't jump. I just turned to slump against the back of the stable. Titus was already a problem. But I still wanted to protect the magi. Even the stupid ones.

"No," I said.

"A lot of frightened people have come up to me to request meetings," he said, leaning against the stable wall beside me. "They want to know what I'm going to do if there are magi here."

I drew in a breath and raised my chin.

"I've avoided drawing a hard line so far," he said.

We didn't have a lot of rules. The important ones fit on a single piece of parchment posted outside the fort.

Work hard to the best of your abilities.

Respect your neighbor and his beliefs.

Protect the settlement the best way you know how.

He hadn't written down "no magic."

"It wouldn't solve the problem," I said, pushing off from the stable wall. "Please don't vilify us for something we didn't choose."

He winced.

His guilt stabbed at me, and I backed up a step. Maybe I shouldn't have been so direct. It wasn't time to be direct if he still felt guilty about sending me to the Forge.

"You keep us safe," I said quietly. "I'll take care of Titus."

CHAPTER TEN

Valens pulled aside a thick fall of vines, revealing a narrow passage through the rocky hill a little like Cassian's necropolis, but clearly better built. The stone around the entrance had been worn smooth and shaped into two posts and a lintel with a set of swords carved into it.

"An outpost for the legion," I said as Valens secured the vines so they wouldn't fall in our way. I squinted at the surrounding greenery edging the river. Grassland stretched on either side and no one would think to look for a cave here among the rolling hills.

"Yes," he said. "But I asked you here because it seems to have something to do with the magi." He tapped the stone framing the entrance, fingers drumming an uneasy cadence. "Seemed important, and I thought you should take a look at it before I tried taking anything back to the fort."

We really needed a better name. We couldn't keep calling our home "the fort." It just didn't sound welcoming.

"All right," I said. I glanced back at Cassian and Titus,

who stood on the rocky ground below us. Valens might have wanted my opinion on an old outpost, but I'd wanted Titus to see the collapse for himself, firsthand. Maybe then he'd understand why we couldn't build our new society the same way again. And I'd asked Cassian to come with us because his presence was soothing to even the most frenetic of our residents. His placid countenance never changed, no matter what emotion or hardship was thrown his way.

I beckoned the other two closer as Valens ducked into the entrance and lit a torch with a bit of flint. Since he and Quintes were the ones who volunteered for scavenging duty most often, he'd come prepared. He passed back a couple more torches and adjusted his belt, where he'd tied some empty sacks to carry anything useful he found.

I followed him into the earth, raising my torch so its light flickered across the smooth stone walls. The cave had obviously started out natural but had been shaped with magic over time. Most of it should be intact, so long as the legion hadn't cut corners and used magic to keep the roof up. But Valens wouldn't have brought us here if he hadn't already decided it was safe.

The narrow passage only lasted a few hundred paces before opening up into a series of caverns separated by hills of stalagmites. Here was the evidence I wanted Titus to see. The rise and subsequent destruction of civilization had left this first room strewn with debris. Racks of weapons and armor had collapsed when the magic holding them together went out. Weapons scattered across the dusty floor mixed with pieces of broken furniture.

"This used to be a ready room," Valens said, moving deeper into the ruin.

I frowned. "Why weren't these put together normally? Most of the furniture in the fort was still intact."

"Because this wasn't a normal outpost. Otherwise, it would have been built outside on a hill where it could intimidate enemies."

"What is it then?"

"That's what I hope we find out."

Titus tripped over a breastplate emblazoned with the crest of the legion. I stepped carefully through the debris, placing my feet with care. It would be easy to turn an ankle in here. Valens and I moved into the next chamber and stopped to stare. If I'd thought the ready room was bad...

Wreckage lay strewn across the cave floor. We had to wade through the remains of furniture and work-stations, clothes, and debris that could have once been food. I knelt to pick up a vivid blue swathe of fabric, half rotted away. On the edge of what might have once been a sleeve, there was a stain where an insignia might have been worn once. I could just make out the stretching flames of magic that would have marked its owner.

My brow furrowed, and I glanced around at all the bits of blue lying in the wreckage. "There were a lot of magi here. Almost an entire division's worth. Was that even a thing? Entire divisions of magi?" That would explain why everything had been held together by magic.

Valens nodded slowly. "Sometimes. They were usually brought in to subdue riots nonlethally. Or...there were rumors of hidden facilities for research and weapon development."

Titus perked up at that, and he stared around with wide eyes. "I thought most magi worked in the city."

"They did." I picked through the debris looking for anything useful. "But they were also stationed with the legion to move troops, relay orders, and wage magical war."

Titus's eyes sparkled. He picked up a length of the blue fabric reserved for the magi and ran the silky cloth through his fingers. Then he held it up to himself to see how it looked.

I snatched it out of his hands. "Look around. I want you to see if you can find anything that is even remotely intact." Maybe then he'd see what kind of destruction our reliance on magic had wrought.

We traveled from room to room, searching through the ruins. Valens found the mess hall and tucked a few plates and forks in his pack. He shrugged when I looked at him funny. "I'm still looking for a complete set for Max and Helena."

The main sections of the cavern were still open except for the debris from all the furnishings. But we found side rooms where ceilings and walls had collapsed, rocks tumbled over each other. In a few of them, skeletons sprawled beneath, swathed in bits of blue fabric.

Titus didn't see destruction everywhere we looked. He only saw the power and the prestige.

"These robes are so fine," he said. "I can't believe they wore these every day."

"Look at this. They each had their own rooms. Their own bathrooms. They carved them out of the rock itself."

"The magi were in charge of this facility," he said,

reading from a logbook he'd found under the rubble. "They weren't even under orders. They were the ones giving the orders to the legion."

"And they died," I snapped. "They're dead Titus. Doesn't that mean anything to you?"

He shrugged. "There's nothing I can do about it."

I stalked away into the very last cavern. Rocks and dirt tumbled in the middle as if a piece of the roof had collapsed under its own weight. Along the edges of the room were the remains of several tables, smashed glassware, and stains where the magi had clearly been working before the Darkness.

Along the back wall, I found a tabletop, intact only because it had been bolted to the wall.

My brow furrowed. For extra protection? I stepped closer.

A large glass container, shaped like a spiraling stem stood clamped to the workspace. The spreading crystal petals beckoned me to touch them, but I kept my hands locked under my armpits.

"What is it?" Valens said. "It's the only thing in here in one piece."

I shook my head. "I don't know. It doesn't look like anything I ever saw at the Forge. But if this facility was here to research new techniques, then I wouldn't recognize it." I'd grown used to the sparks of vytl throughout the world. It moved in this cave the same way it moved everywhere else. But here by the table little eddies and whirls of light circled the glass flower, almost like the petals were a funnel but the power couldn't seem to find a way in.

"A weapon maybe?" Titus said. "That seems like what they were working on."

Cassian made his way around the rubble. "If that's the case, it is most likely dangerous."

I nodded even as my brother moved a little closer. He flipped through a pile of notes that lay loosely bound on the bench beside the object.

"Not a weapon," he said, voice hushed. "It's a device. For controlling troops."

I blinked. "Like communicating with them."

"No, controlling them. From inside their minds. It says that if you fill it with power, it will make troops fight without question. They will advance until the enemy is dead or they are."

My mouth dropped open, and Valens stepped away from the thing, mouth twisted with horror. My family were soldiers. They'd fought for the Empire whole heartedly so the very idea of being forced seemed invasive and foreign.

We'd grown up hearing about the glory of the Empire and the legion that defended it. But what happened in those far-off provinces that hadn't been quite quelled? Where the locals were still fighting back. This device would turn any magi into a general or a commander and any raw untrained recruits into unstoppable fighting machines.

Did it work on non-fighters as well? Could you use this to take over the minds of anyone you wanted?

"We have to destroy it," I said.

Cassian nodded emphatically.

"What?" Titus cried. "Are you serious? You want to destroy the last creation from the greatest magi? You can't!"

"This is an atrocity," I said. "If the Empire planned to use this, then I'm glad it fell before it could."

Titus brought his hands together. "No, think about how useful it could be. We could use it in the fort. No one will ever argue about what has to be done first ever again. You could make them all realize what's important and they would do it."

"Like farming?" I said, rounding on him. "What if someone made you dig in the dirt even if you didn't want to? All day, every day against your will. How would that make you feel?"

"That wouldn't happen," he said, retreating a step. "I'm magi. And the magi would be in charge."

Valens gasped, and I fought down a sigh. Trust Titus to blow his most important secret without a second thought.

"We're the ones who can use the device," Titus said. "And we're more powerful. We're more important."

I opened my mouth but I couldn't form the words for why that made my skin crawl. It wasn't just because the world ended because of the magi.

The magi had put me through hell in the Forge. Just so I could be Tempered. Just so I could have this power I was too afraid to use.

I didn't want anyone who was that good at hurting other people to be in charge of anything.

I shook my head. "We're destroying it. We're not building ourselves up based on that kind of power. Not this time."

His lips thinned, and his eyes hardened. "I'm not letting you do that. This is so much better than what we have."

He reached for the clamp to free the device.

Valens was way ahead of him, swinging a table leg against the glass.

Instead of shattering, it rang, clear and cold, and the table leg fell from my brother's hand as he cried out in pain.

Titus growled and swept his hand through the air. He didn't even touch Valens, but my brother, the experienced legionnaire went flying.

"Valens!" I called, but Titus turned on me.

Cassian threw himself on Titus but a blast of air thrust him into me.

As Titus raised his hands, I put my arms around Cassian. Vytl flowed toward Titus, traveling up his limbs to pour into his chest. I pushed out with my mind, just as Titus sent a blast of raw power over us.

Heat surged around my makeshift shield, sizzling as power met power.

"Thank you," Cassian said in my ear. "How long can you hold it?"

"I have no idea," I shouted back. "I'm making this up as I go."

I held him until Titus's attack ran out, then I stepped away and flung up my own hands. I had no idea what I was doing. My own magic was based on nothing more than instinct and book knowledge. I knew the basics of a magi's skill, but I had no experience to draw on.

I yanked up from the ground, pulling anything I could get a grip on, and rocks tore up from the cavern floor, knocking Titus on his ass.

I panted and raced for the device on the table.

With a wordless cry, Titus sat up and pushed a hand out

toward me. Something solid and cold hit me in the middle and with a boom, I was flung back into the wall.

My head cracked against the stone as Cassian landed beside me in a heap.

The cavern swung, tilting precariously as I tried to find which way was up and which way was down. My stomach heaved.

The light from our forgotten torches blurred around Titus's figure as he stepped close to kneel before me. I tried to grab him. But my head spun and he split into two. I couldn't even tell which one I wanted to spit at.

"You told me I couldn't make decisions for everyone else. So, I'm making this one for myself," he said.

Both versions of him walked to the table to pick up the device and the papers that went with it.

He looked between the device and me and the papers before tucking the notes in his tunic. "I'll figure out how to use it later."

He stopped beside the opening to the rest of the facility to look back at me, then disappeared through the doorway.

CHAPTER ELEVEN

Papa didn't waste time on stupid questions like "how could you let this happen?" and "what were you thinking?" He stood in front of the rough desk Quintes had made with his back straight and his arms crossed, eyes on the wall behind us. This side of the barracks had been converted into his office.

"What is Titus likely to do now?" he said. "What can we expect? What can we do to prepare?"

I chewed my lip and glanced at Valens, but my brother was already looking at me expectantly. I rubbed my palms against my skirt, leaving smears of sweat. "I think having magic made Titus feel special," I said. "He idolizes the old magi and the old way of doing things. I think he liked the idea of having a place in that society. He wants the prestige and the respect magic would have given him in the Empire."

Cassian stared straight ahead. "And now he has a device that can force people to give him exactly that." His voice was as even as ever but his thumb rubbed a frayed seam in his robes over and over again.

I reached across to still his fingers. "Best case, he'll probably try to build a society with himself at the top. Worst case...he'll try to take over the fort and steal everything we've built so far."

Papa took a deep breath through his nose and rubbed his temples. "Whatever he chooses, it will likely bring us into conflict with him again."

Valens growled. "If he's smart, he'll run as far away as he can with what he's stolen."

"We can't count on that." Papa shook his head and dropped his arms, and suddenly I was looking at the Archgeneral and not my father. "Valens, fetch Max and Decima. We'll lay plans for every scenario. Whatever he chooses, we'll be ready."

My brother stood and hesitated, like he just kept himself from saluting, before he ran for the door.

I tightened my grip on Cassian's hand to keep my fingers from trembling. I hated the nausea that sent bile up the back of my throat. I hated that I felt this sick about talking to my father. I'd always been able to say anything to him. Anything except this, but the thought had been ricocheting around my skull since Titus had smacked me into the wall, and putting it off wouldn't make it any easier.

"We can't destroy the device by normal means," I blurted.

Papa focused on me.

"We tried already. Valens's blow just bounced right off. It's protected somehow. If Titus uses it, then the only way to beat him is to use magic."

"No," Papa said.

I jerked. "You haven't even heard what I was going to say."

"Magic is what got us into this trouble."

"We can't avoid it anymore." I stood, letting go of Cassian's hand. My chair scraped across the flagstones. "There will be more like Titus. Magi who were made after the world fell. Hardship will always make new ones whether you like it or not. The solution is not to ignore us."

Maybe if I'd let Titus build something, if I'd let him help, it might have kept him from this path. Maybe he would have learned moderation and humility, rather than seeing magic as some sort of right I'd been keeping from him.

"Your magic didn't do any good against Titus today," Papa said, lowering his chin to meet my eyes.

"That's because I have no practice using it," I snapped. "If I concentrate on learning, I can protect us from him."

"No."

I took an involuntary step back and swallowed. I rarely heard that tone of voice from him. Not since I'd been little and had a penchant for stealing cookies.

He shook his head as if to soften the blow. "This isn't just about building a new society without any reliance on magic. This is about the attitude of our people. They're scared. And they're not happy about magi being in the fort. I can see what will happen if we try to force them to accept this. And I'm worried you'll get hurt if people know you're a magi."

The hairs along my arms raised because I knew he was right. But I knew I couldn't do anything else now. "I can protect myself," I said.

"Aurelia. Don't put this settlement in that position."

I flushed. He said it because if I was in danger, my family would protect me no matter the cost. They'd choose me over the rest of our people.

But I would have forced them to choose.

My heart hammered as I stared at my father. He wanted so desperately for me to be someone I wasn't. He wanted me to be someone who wasn't a magi. Or at the very least, someone who could forget they were a magi.

"Promise me," he said. He didn't yell, he didn't demand. He asked.

I couldn't unclench my jaw. So I lowered my head and nodded.

"Thank you." The toes of his boots came into view. He needed new ones. The last pair his size that we'd come across he'd given to Renallius.

He put his hands on my shoulders. "We'll find some other way to counter Titus. Some mundane way that won't compromise what we've built and won't put you in danger."

I barely kept myself from flinching. I was a compromise.

By not accepting what I was, by pushing the issue under the rug, he was saying I didn't belong here. There wasn't a place for me in this new society they were building.

"Of course we will," I said. It was the first time I'd lied to my father since those long-ago cookie days.

I spun away and out the door, fleeing his misunderstanding protectiveness and my falsehood.

"Aurelia." Cassian caught up to me at the corner of the barracks, but only because I stopped abruptly enough he almost ran over me. I pulled my cloak closer. The night air bit as it moved past my bare arms.

"Aurelia," Cassian started, and I swung around to face him.

"What's wrong with me?" I cried.

"I don't know," he said, answering the question I'd asked and not the one I meant.

"Why can't I just do what the others all want? Why can't I bury this part of me? Every time I try, it comes bursting out in moments of panic. Or...or I think too much and I feel hopeless and like half a person."

"You can't bury it because it's a piece of you?" he said, voice raised as if he wasn't sure about what he was saying. "You can't cut off a piece of your heart and live without it. Or, or a hand. Or maybe you could. I don't know a magi's power all that well. How many limbs could you chop off and still live?"

His mumbling released a bit of my wound-up tension and I laughed in spite of myself.

His hands fluttered at his sides, and he looked down at them for a moment. "Would it make you feel better if I embraced you?"

"A hug, Cassian," I said with another laugh. "It's called a hug. And it would only make me feel better if you actually want to hug me."

"Oh, that's easy then." He reached out and drew me into his broad chest. My hands slipped up the smooth surface of his robe to grip his shoulders.

"I hated every minute in the Forge," I said into his chest.

"Nine months of torment. So why do I want to use it so much? Why is it so bad if I don't?"

"If you don't, your time there meant nothing," Cassian said as if stating a fact. It was what he always did. He answered the surface because that was what he felt safe understanding. But these words reached deeper than my surface. They reached to the very heart of my anguish and pulled it out so I could look at it.

"If I don't use my power, then my suffering means nothing." I kept my head down as my heart raced in recognition. "If we don't talk about what I went through, then it's like I didn't go through it. But I did. I did and it changed me."

"You can't go back to who you were before," he said, chest rumbling under my forehead. He would know. He couldn't go back to who he was before the Darkness either. None of us could.

"No. But I can keep moving and be someone even better." Someone without that uncertainty and heartache.

It would break my father's heart.

He was already breaking mine.

I pushed away from Cassian and brushed my eyes with hands that trembled. "Thank you. I know what to do now."

"I'm glad."

The fort was dark, with only soft huffs coming from the stables. Candles were precious and torches made us an easy target for bandits so when the sun went down, most people went to sleep. But I knew one person who'd be awake.

I knocked on the door made from the flattened-out slats of a barrel.

Helena answered, her belly just getting round enough to

notice through her dress. "I'm sorry to bother you," I said. "But I knew you'd probably be awake anyway."

"You mean you knew I'd probably be puking anyway." She gestured me inside.

"Is Max here?"

"No, Valens came and told him your father needed him."

I turned in the tight quarters, which still smelled like sawdust. The low ceiling made the little house feel claustrophobic but at least it kept out the spring rains. "Good. I need your help."

Helena listened, face still, hands clenched while I explained. And in her defense, she never once interrupted.

"I need you to teach me. I can't be unprepared again."

Her breath released in a slow sigh. "You're asking me to lie to my husband and my father-in-law." She spoke quietly. The single-family houses were built close enough together you could hear when your neighbors had an argument.

"We're already lying to them," I said, keeping my voice down, too. "We're already pretending that we aren't magi. Well, we are magi, Helena. So is Titus. And you can bet he isn't pretending anymore."

She stood and paced to the bed. Five meager steps. "I was a battle magi," she said. "A tool of the legion. I transported troops. I delivered messages. I killed people. I don't know anything about that device you found."

I sensed her caving, and I pressed the advantage. "I'll figure that out on my own. It's the practical side of things I need. The only thing I know about magic is from books and lectures at the Forge. You know that's only going to get me so far." Mostly it had gotten me pummeled by Titus.

She stood in the dark, head bowed. She was either staring at her belly or staring at her bed. I couldn't tell which.

"If Titus comes here, he threatens everything we've built. And Papa doesn't know what he's capable of. None of us know what a magi can do who wasn't Tempered or trained in the Forge. We need someone who can counter him."

"Max can't find out," she said, then turned and sought my eyes in the dark. "This is your path, not mine. I was content to move on."

I stood and placed my fist over my heart in the style of the old Empire. We didn't have anything that carried as much weight in our new world. "I so swear."

She put her hands on her hips. "Fine," she said, voice quiet but steady. "Fine. We'll start with drawing power."

CHAPTER TWELVE

We usually practiced as far away from Namar as we
could safely walk in an hour.

I waited till we'd dropped our baskets in a meadow on the
far side of Cassian's necropolis before I turned to give Helena
her present.

She gasped as she pulled the cloth back. "Are these...are
these cookies?"

"I hope so. Claudia was trying to trade out smooshed
apples for sugar so I don't know if they'll be any good—"

Helena shoved one into her mouth whole before I could
finish, and her eyes rolled back in her head. "Mmf, perfect."

"I guess so," I said, raising my eyebrows.

"Shut up. This baby wants sweets. And no one wants to
spare what little we have on pregnancy cravings. And all the
grannies just want to shove me full of meat and vegetables."
She ran her hands down her belly. She might have been very
round, but she still moved with a grace I envied.

"Well, I wanted you to have something special. I know you don't really like what we're doing."

She sighed and ducked to grab her basket. "I had a much harder time convincing Max to let me leave the settlement today. He only agreed because I told him everyone has to help out if we're going to make it through the next winter. And I promised him you'd be with me."

"Huh, I have done some training with Decima. Maybe he thinks my blade work is better now."

"It's more likely he had a look at your lists and didn't like the numbers."

My lips twisted, and I glanced around the meadow. A bend of the river carved through the tall grasses supporting bushes of berries and several large clumps of edible greens. Namar grew every month. Having more people around meant we had more hands for farming, foraging, and defense, but it also meant more mouths to feed. I still did all the math, running through projections for the next season, trying to figure out how much we would need. Especially since more people always joined us in the winter.

I blew out my breath in a guilty sigh. I'd escaped the numbers a little earlier than I should have today. But if I was honest with myself, I'd never found my work very satisfying. It needed to be done, sure. And I was decent at it. But it didn't feel like what I was supposed to be doing.

I ran my hands down my left leg, rubbing out the soreness. With all the work up at the fort, I hardly had to walk this far anymore.

"How are you doing?" I asked as my sister-in-law found

herself a patch of berry bushes where she could sit and fill her basket. "Still tired?"

"I've been tired since the Darkness," she said. "It's hard to notice a difference. But I still feel all right. No more nausea and I can still get off the ground, so that's good news. The Empire would have sent me home from my post by now."

"Good to know they were concerned for their magi's health," I said.

She snorted. "They were more concerned about results and there were plenty more magi waiting to take my place who wouldn't have been as distracted. I prefer this. Max wants to wrap me up in gauze, but it's nice feeling like I'm actually doing something to help."

"You're definitely helping me."

She nodded decisively. "Is anyone coming?"

I stood on my toes to survey the wide plains around us. The fort bustled on the horizon, but the area around us was clear. I couldn't see Valens or Quintes with either of their scavenging parties, and all the hunters were supposed to be to the east today.

Helena sat on the riverbank collecting berries and bushels of watercress and rampion while I practiced to the soothing sound of her instruction.

"The hardest part about magic is that it's mostly instinctive. It's the body's natural defense, so of course the body wants to defend itself. Your body wants to use magic when it feels threatened."

I exhaled, concentrating on the fine lines of vytl flowing through the meadow, wrapping around Helena and I like it recognized us.

"But all energy in the world is volatile in some way, including vytl. If you draw too much at a time or draw it too fast, you're more likely to hurt yourself or everyone around you. A magi's strength lies in their control."

The vytl flowed in and through me with the barest call. She was right. It was instinctive, and if I reached, more poured into me, answering my call. I focused on drawing power evenly, along with my breath.

A berry smacked me in the face and I jumped. The surrounding vytl reacted, pulsing in time with my thumping heart, and it shot into my skin. I yelped and pulled back from the sting.

I cracked an eye open to see Helena muffling a laugh. "See?"

I glared. "What was that for?"

"I'm teaching you control. Drawing vytl is instinctive. You now have to get to the point where controlling that draw is instinctive as well."

I rubbed my forehead. I probably had a stain marking the lesson. "How did the Empire teach magi control?"

She sobered. "You don't want to know."

I thought of the Forge and shuddered. She was right, I didn't.

I continued to practice while she pelted me with bits of grass and dirt, trying to distract me. I felt like I was doing pretty well until I got a face full of river water.

I spluttered. "Hey!" I shook water from my eyes and lurched upright. My hands closed on some loose bits of grass lying around me and I threw them back at her. "How do you like it?"

She laughed and fell over clutching her sides. "Oh, but you made the funniest face."

I opened my mouth to respond but movement caught my eye now that I was standing. Figures milled beside the next bend of the river, and I gasped and ducked.

Helena immediately sat up, her mouth tight. "What is it?"

"Scavengers."

"Ours?"

I shook my head.

She lowered her voice. "Who would be working around here? The settlers from Abele's farm don't come out this far."

"I don't know. I think we should check."

We crept closer, enough to hear the sound of their movements and water lapping the sides of a boat. But no voices.

"Why aren't they speaking?" I whispered.

Helena just shook her head and crept closer. We stayed near the riverbank where more screening shrubbery grew. She tiptoed through the mud as if she wasn't carrying a half-grown person around and crouched where we had a good view of the group.

Three men with scruffy beards and clothes held together with rope clambered onto a makeshift raft. These looked like loners. In the two and a half years since the Darkness, most people had at least learned how to put their clothes back together. Since these hadn't, they probably hadn't settled in one place long enough to figure it out.

Beside me, Helena drew in a quick breath.

"What is it?" I said.

"There's something odd about them. Look at the vytl as it moves around them."

I squinted but didn't see anything. Less vytl moved over the water, maybe that was the problem. "Is it odd enough we should follow them?"

She bit her lip. "I think so. Max will yell, but I think your father is going to need to know about them."

That raft of theirs hadn't been built for long journeys otherwise I wouldn't have suggested it. But we managed to keep up along the riverbank. There were a couple of places where we managed to get ahead by cutting straight across a wide meander of the river.

"Oh no," I said as we came around the last bend.

"Did they see us?"

"No. I just recognize this place."

We couldn't get close enough to actually see it, not without being seen ourselves, but the hill rose before us and I knew that around the other side there would be an opening between the rocks screened by vines.

I got down on my belly and looked out over the river where the men pulled up their raft. Helena crouched beside me, staying in the shrubs. As soon as they stepped on land, I could see what Helena had been talking about. Vytl flowed around them as usual except near their heads where it collected in a fuzzy jagged halo. Not like a magi, where it chose to congregate, but almost like it was trapped and angry about it.

They disappeared into the cave where we'd found the device.

I rolled over onto my back and blew out my breath. "It's Titus."

She glanced sharply at the riverbank. "It is?"

"This is where we found the device. It wouldn't surprise me if he took over the facility."

"And he's gathering a force to support him," she said. "Did you see how the power moved around them?"

"Like it was chaining them."

"I think we're seeing the device in action. Those men were not free."

"I wish we could get inside to see how many he had already. And what he's doing with them."

Her mouth fell open. "You're not actually going to sneak in there, are you?"

I scoffed. "No, of course not. I'm not stupid. We're going to retreat. At least now we know where Titus is. And whatever he's up to, he still has to get ready for winter, too. Maybe that will be enough to keep him busy for a while."

CHAPTER THIRTEEN

I used to think fear would diminish as our position became more stable. I did not think how it would change and morph into something new.

The fears that drove us in the beginning—starvation, lack of shelter, bandits—slid aside as they were solved only to make room for other fears like discovery and the threat to everything we'd built.

Cassian sat on a bunk in the back corner of the barracks, opposite Papa's office. We'd turned the space into the healer's quarters by hanging a curtain from the roof.

Breva, as old as Granmamma and just as capable, pushed past Papa and Max to dab some cream on Cassian's split lip. His arm had already been splinted and there wasn't a lot else that could be done for the bruising we couldn't see under his robes.

"How many were there?" Papa asked, hands locked on his belt.

"Two," Cassian replied. "They thought Vitruven was a magi. They followed him between the barn and the wall and jumped him there in the dark."

"And you followed."

"I could not walk away."

He kept his voice even, but his hands trembled, and I wondered how close to the surface his panic lay. How similar was this beating to all the ones he'd taken from his division? I put my hand on the bunk beside him so he could grasp it if he wanted. He placed his good hand over my fingers.

"We got there minutes later to break up the fight," Decima said, standing on the other side of the bed. "But not soon enough to prevent any injuries."

"How is Vitruven?" Papa asked the old healer.

She snorted. "In better shape than this one. I sent him home to his wife already."

"What are we going to do about this?" Max said hands slicing through the air. "They attacked two of their neighbors. Just because they thought one might be a magi."

Papa stared at the evidence of Cassian's assault for a heartbeat or two and I drew a breath, waiting for his decision.

"We don't have a choice in the matter," he said. "We cannot allow someone to stay here who would attack another person. Whether that person is magi or not."

I swallowed and let the breath go. For a moment, I was worried Papa was going to make the punishment dependent on who the victim was. I couldn't help the way my mind raced down that track. I could see the future as clearly as Papa sometimes. If he'd declared the attackers protected because they'd been justified, or he'd only given them some sort of work detail, none of the magi in the settlement would have felt safe again.

They already didn't feel safe, but at least I could still convince them that Papa would protect everyone.

As long as they kept their magic hidden.

"Decima," Papa said, voice firm. "Collect the culprits in the tower. We will hear their side of the story and determine our verdict. If everything matches up, and they really did attack someone for nothing more than a suspicion about who they were before the Darkness, then we will have to make this a formal exile. We have to set a precedent."

Decima snapped off a smart salute and turned on her heel. Max followed her. Decima's squad had arrived in time to keep Cassian from anything worse than broken bones and bruises, but she blamed herself that he'd been hurt at all.

With my siblings gone and Breva wrapping up her tools and bandages, I scooted my chair closer to Cassian's side. Papa remained silent for a moment before speaking.

"Is Vitruven a magi?" he said quietly to the foot of Cassian's bed.

I kept my gaze fixed on the blankets. "No." That was the worst part. Vitruven was just some settler with more luck than most. The power in the world moved around him as it did everyone without magic.

Breva moved off as Papa took a step forward.

"But you know who they are."

My hands clenched and Cassian winced. I forced myself to relax my fingers, but my shoulders remained tense. "I know all of them."

I waited, jaw tight, for him to ask me to name them. I waited till I would have to say no.

He didn't ask. Finally, after waiting for me to do something other than stare at the bed, he left the barracks, and I could meet Cassian's eyes.

"What are you going to do?" he said.

I rubbed my face. "Nothing. At least, nothing more than I'm already doing. The magi aren't going anywhere. This is our home, too. We helped build it."

"Will any of them help defend it with you?"

"I don't know," I said quietly. "I can't make that decision for them. A lot of them are done with violence."

Cassian closed his eyes and leaned back against the straw-stuffed pillow.

"I wonder if I could convince you to be done with violence, too."

He cracked an eye to give me a look. "If you want to defend your home and your people, you cannot condemn me for doing the same."

"No. I can't." Not when it meant so much to him. Not when it meant how much he'd changed so that he could choose to defend. "I'm proud of you. And at the same time, I'm scared to death you're going to get yourself killed." I held his hand, but it wasn't enough. "May I hold you?"

"Please."

I climbed into the bunk beside him. He lifted his good

arm so I could stretch out and put my hand on his chest. His heartbeat against my palm was comforting.

He didn't think he was worth fighting for, but he'd defend me, he'd defend his fellow settlers to the death.

"Do you pray?" He stood at the top of the tower every morning to watch the sun, but I never asked what was in his head or his heart when he gathered with the other settlers that wanted the company of a Keeper.

"Not for myself," he said. His arm tightened around me. "But I pray for you all the time."

"Then I'll pray for you, myself. That should even things out."

"You don't have to."

"I want to."

His breath hitched under my hand but he didn't protest.

Maybe if I showed him he was worth it to me, he'd eventually believe it himself.

Mamma let the stored grain trickle through her fingers back into the bag as she stared around the storehouse with consternation.

"There were fifteen sacks of grain a week ago," she said. "Now there are five. There were thirteen crates of vegetables."

"Now there are four," I said. I double-checked her numbers against my list. "You're right. This isn't a mistake in our records. This is theft."

"Let's be careful with that accusation," Claudia said quietly. "It's a serious one."

Especially in a settlement like this where everyone knew their neighbors as well as they knew their own family. But I was very careful with my numbers and they weren't lying.

"I don't know what else to call it," I said. "Siphoning? Pilfering? Do we even know who is doing the taking? Or where they could be taking it? This is a lot of food. Two-thirds of our winter stores. If it was one person, why would they be trying to feed an army?"

My throat closed as I realized who this sounded like. The stealing, the disregard for anyone else. The building of an army.

"I don't know," Mamma said, not following my thoughts. She stood and brushed her hands down her uniform. The ill-made rushlights in the wall sconces flickered. We'd converted the stable into a storehouse in the late summer when it had seemed like we'd have plenty to get us through the winter. Or at least enough.

This changed things.

"Whoever it is has taken food out of the mouths of their neighbors," she said, putting her hands on her hips. "They've jeopardized everyone's survival. How will we get them all through the winter?" She rubbed her forehead.

I was already scribbling more numbers, dividing by way too many people, when Decima pushed through the door.

"We found the thief," she said, breathless.

"What, already?" Claudia dropped the empty sack she'd been holding.

"We need Aurelia."

My mouth dropped open as I met her eyes. Why would Decima's guards need me? They were all competent soldiers even compared to my family.

Unless this thief had some sort of magic.

A sinking feeling grew in my gut as I abandoned my notebook and hurried after Decima, my gait uneven. It wouldn't be one of my magi. None of them would ever draw attention to themselves this way. But Titus would have no problem with it.

She led me out the gates into a crisp clear winter morning. We hadn't had a lot of snow yet this winter so the grass bent brittle and brown under our feet.

We passed groups working to build a barn beside the walls and another couple of people worked on the roof of Cassian's new chapel. This winter with its mild weather had been a wonderful time to get some more buildings up, especially as we'd grown too big to hold everyone inside the walls.

Several people stopped to stare as we raced past. I recognized Renallius's wide eyes and a couple of others that dropped their tools in surprise.

At the far edge of our settlement, Decima's guards arrayed themselves in a line behind Papa, who stood with his hands out and his face set in hard lines. A woman with lank blonde hair and a slack expression wavered before him.

I recognized her, but only just. She'd come in the last wave of newcomers and besides getting her work assignment from me she hadn't spoken to anyone as far as I knew. She slept in one of the communal bunkhouses and worked with Claudia without complaint.

She stepped slowly and steadily with a sack of corn slung over her shoulder, eyes blank and staring straight ahead.

"Stop, now," Papa said, trying to block her without actually bringing any of his strength against her. "I don't want to have to hurt you."

She didn't even acknowledge him, she just continued to trudge steadily down the hill, veering around obstacles. That's when I noticed the halo of power swirling around her head. Titus.

Decima pulled her sword and joined her soldiers. "If you don't stop, we will be forced to kill you."

I lunged forward and pulled her arm down, pointing her sword at the ground. "Stop. She's not in control of herself."

"This is Titus's doing?" Papa said with a growl.

"We can't just let him walk off with our supplies," Decima said and stepped as if to intercept the woman again.

"No, but threats won't work," I said. "The device was designed to walk troops into battle. I doubt any kind of violence will keep them from their goal."

Could I just reach out and snap Titus's connection with the woman? Surely it would be more complicated than that. The magic was designed by magi who were used to battle and espionage.

I wished Helena was here. Between the two of us, we might be able to come up with something. But she was home with Max, tending their new baby.

My lips thinned. She wouldn't want to be a part of this anyway. And if I could handle this on my own, then she wouldn't have to be.

"She's not in control of herself," I said again. "But I think I can help her." I could at least try.

I raised my hands.

Papa lunged forward and grabbed my wrists. "No," he said, voice dark and rough. "Not with all of them watching. You'll show everyone what you are."

His fingers dug into my skin, and I realized it wasn't just Decima's guards anymore. Behind us, a group had gathered. I recognized each face. Every one of them magi, waiting, watching me as their hands clenched and feet shifted.

They'd seen me running, and they'd assumed the worst. The magi were frightened, terrified of revealing themselves, but they'd come anyway. To help me if I needed it.

The woman kept walking, slowly but surely stealing our supplies. One of Decima's guards reversed his blade and lunged to knock the woman's feet out from under her.

Her apathy fled. She leaped aside and swift as the wind, swung her sack against the guard's head. Then she drew her knife from her belt.

I pulled my hands from my father's grip and raised them again, but Papa thrust me behind him and gave Decima a signal I recognized. Terminate.

I sucked in a breath. Even Decima hesitated, her face reflecting horror.

"No," I cried, then I rounded on my father. "You'd rather kill an innocent woman than see me use magic?" I hissed under my breath. I shook my head. "Who are you? My father would never make that choice."

He jerked and moved back a step. His chest heaved as his

eyes darted between me and the woman and Decima. Like he only just realized what he was doing.

He gave Decima the signal to strike the last order. "Restrain her," he said. "Place her in the cells. We will not allow someone to take our people as well as our food. If she fights, use non-lethal force to confine her." His hand slashed through the air. "Lock down the stores. Anyone caught stealing food will go into confinement."

Decima and her guards moved to comply.

They left Papa and me standing on the hill of dead grass, staring at each other. I drew in a breath that shuddered. My chest ached when I looked at his face. He loved me so much and didn't understand me at all. His fear for me would have driven him to make a choice that would have broken him. Killing that woman would have changed him into someone I didn't recognize.

But I didn't know how to fix what was between us. I couldn't just tell him not to be afraid. He'd seen the fall of the Empire. He'd seen what our neighbors had done to a man they only suspected was a magi.

But I refused to live in fear as well. I was not going to be afraid of myself or the people around me.

He turned away before I could catch him and try to explain. Before we could do anything to fix this.

His gaze settled on the crowd. The magi who lived in hiding but risked exposure to see which way their future was going to go.

"Go home," he said, voice carrying with a forced note of casualness. "Go back to work. The matter has been resolved."

They didn't look at him. They looked at me.

I gave them a tiny nod. They faded back toward the buildings and the fort, but not before my father noticed the exchange.

He glanced at me, opened his mouth to demand an explanation, and I walked away.

I was already thinking about what I would have to do to protect the settlement. Without my father's knowledge.

CHAPTER FOURTEEN

That night the magi gathered in one of the homes outside the walls. Renallius had offered his house mostly because his wife was also a magi. They didn't have to worry about hiding anything from each other, just from their neighbors.

These newer houses were much better built than the ones within the walls since we'd had more practice, but I was pretty sure the whole thing would collapse if we packed anyone else in here. Thirteen of them sat around the tiny space, lining the bed, crowded on the floor, propped up against the walls. Helena sat beside me on one of the few chairs, my new niece in her arms.

I stood with my rear end propped against the table and surveyed my people. They waited, tense and quiet, eyes trained on me.

"Titus has finally moved directly against us," I said.

"The thefts?" Renallius said, running a hand over his bald pate. "They're him, aren't they?"

"Yes. Titus has been stealing our food stores. But worse, I think he's been stealing our people as well."

A rumble went through the gathered magi as they glanced at each other, murmuring questions and worries.

The door banged, making everyone jump, but it was Cassian who poked his head in the crack and let himself into the meeting. A couple of magi glanced at him suspiciously, but when I nodded at him in welcome, they allowed themselves to relax a little.

"I've been over the whole settlement now, and there are two others missing. Beanus and Gloria." The two had been more loners. Aside from getting their work assignments from me, they hadn't really fit in or made any friends in the settlement. Their neighbors had told me today that they'd assumed the two had just decided the settlement wasn't for them and left to find something better. My chest felt tight and fluttery when I thought about them. I wished now that we'd gone after them. We were supposed to be a community. An adopted family and we'd just let them walk off.

"If we'd tried to stop them, could we have done anything?" Renallius asked. "Has anyone tried to do anything for the one who was stopped this morning?"

Beside me, Helena shook her head. She'd tried this afternoon. Discreetly. But she'd been interrupted by Decima's guards and hadn't wanted to force the issue.

"Does anyone know how to break the control?" I said. With so many of us, surely, we'd be able to come up with something. "Or have any ideas? Did you all get a good look at it this morning?"

There was a collective murmuring as they all looked at

each other. They'd each been there, watching as I'd confronted Papa. They should have been able to see the woman and the way the magic moved her.

Finally, Renallius shook his head. "I can't think of anything. And without knowing more about how the device works, I don't have any ideas."

No one admitted to having been on the team that developed it.

I hoped that meant that no one here actually had been. I hoped no one here would be selfish enough or so afraid that if they had the answer, they still wouldn't speak up. But I understood why they might not.

"We might need to have access to the actual device to break the control it has," I said, rubbing my forehead. "I wish we'd at least gotten the notes that went with it."

I took a deep breath before I asked the next question. I didn't want to ask it, but I wanted it to be decided, not avoided.

"Is it worth...creating new magi? Like the Empire did. In order to fight Titus."

The temperature in the room dropped as knuckles went white and spines stiffened. Too many gazes dropped until only one or two magi dared to look at me.

"Is it worth putting anyone through what we went through to gain our power?"

"No," Helena said. She raised her chin, arms clutched tight around my niece. "No, it is not."

Renallius stood and faced me with his hands tucked behind his back. "I think I speak for everyone when I say we don't want to be a society that creates trauma for the sake of power. We want to be the type of society that helps people heal."

I closed my eyes as my shoulders sagged. "Yes," I said. "That's what I want as well. Thank you."

There would always be new magi. The world was full of hardship and trauma and new magi would be Tempered from it. But we would never replicate the Forge. We'd never try to break someone just so we could rebuild them stronger.

"Are we going to have to go to war?" another magi said, a young woman with hair down past her shoulders. When she'd come, it had been shorn short in a soldier's cut.

It wasn't an idle question. Many of those here had served in the Empire's legion. They knew what war was like. They'd lived with the constant press of it.

"I don't know," I said. "The general hasn't made anything official. But we will protect our home and our people."

The girl nodded. "I will fight. With sword and shield, with bow and arrows. With every breath I have in me."

But not with magic. They didn't say it, but they didn't want to defend their home with magic if it meant that same home would throw them out after the fight. I met each of their eyes in turn. Every one of them nodded.

I straightened up. "More importantly, I don't think we have enough food to make it through the rest of the winter. Not even if we slaughter all the livestock and start over finding more strays in the spring. I don't know about the rest of you, but I want to find us some more food."

"How?" one of them asked. "It's winter. Nothing's growing. Are you asking us to charm game into our traps?"

I tilted my head. "Is that even possible?"

He opened his mouth and closed it, thinking.

Cassian raised his hand tentatively. "What about the cache?"

"What cache?" Renallius said.

My lips parted. "Every fort has a cache of food stores," I said. "Things that are supposed to be preserved and held in case of emergency. We never found it or cleared it out." Back when we'd first come, I'd been so preoccupied with suppressing what I was that I'd pushed it out of my mind and successfully forgotten about it.

"If magic was used to hide it, wouldn't that magic have disappeared during the Darkness," someone said.

"Unless the magic was just to move something physical, to hide it away behind some sort of mundane barrier," Helena said. "That was done all the time so enemy magi couldn't disrupt the spells."

"Then how will we find it?"

"We ask someone who was here." I turned to Cassian. I didn't want to bring up anything that had happened during the Darkness, but he'd been the one to remember it in the first place.

His fingers drummed against his knee, then nodded to me. "I might be able to find it again. I remember where the magi worked to hide it. But…"

"But?" I said.

"It's in the tower," he said. "We'll have to get past Decima's guards."

I nodded and pushed off the table. "We can do that."

"We will have to use magic," one of the others said. "To

get past the guards. To open the cache. I thought we didn't want to use it ever again."

I opened my mouth but found I had no argument. He was right. But I couldn't find the words to explain that this was different.

Helena stood. "I am willing to use magic to help my neighbors and my family." Her eyes flicked to me. "As long as no one knows about it."

That was the sticking point. The thing that tripped us all up. It wasn't the magic that was the problem. At least not always. It was the reactions of those we loved.

"I am willing as well," I said, making sure my words came out bright and clear.

"We're working against our own people?" Renallius asked.

"We're working *for* our own people," I said. "They just can't know about it. I'll take volunteers only. We might need more than one magi to unseal the cache."

In the end, I had five volunteers, and I had to tell the others to lie low. More than I expected had leaped at the chance to help their settlement. Even if it meant using magic again.

We had to make it through the rest of the fort before we could get to the tower where Decima's guards had set up their barracks and a rudimentary cell block. But a group of magi traipsing through the houses and storerooms within the walls would have attracted attention, so we staggered our arrival at the tower by a few minutes each.

I pressed myself against the wall outside the door next to two of my magi strike force. Cassian joined us, leaning up on the other side of the door. In my head, I counted down. Three, two, one.

Outside the walls, a flash lit up the night sky. Shouts rang from the stone, carrying up through the buildings and the main street.

Renallius creating a distraction.

I was pretty sure he hadn't actually blown anything up, but I'd double-check with him later. The object was to get Decima and most of her guards out of the tower, not damage the settlement.

Helena leaned her head back against the wall as Decima and three others raced through the door of the tower. We held our breath as they passed, but none of them noticed us or even looked over. We were safe in the bubble of silence Helena had created.

The moment the guards had passed out of the door, I slipped in behind them. Per regulation, Decima had left one guard here in the tower to handle any other emergencies that might crop up. He stood as we entered, his mouth opening to ask our business, and I threw a rope of power toward him with a command in my mind.

"Sleep."

Cassian caught the guard as he fell backward over his chair and laid him down with his head on the table as if he'd just fallen asleep where he'd been sitting.

A couple of chairs and the table occupied the space at the

base of the tower. A few bunks were pushed up against the opposite wall beside the stairs to the cellar.

I limped for the steps.

Cell bars had been set into the stone from floor to ceiling, original to the tower, and our brainwashed citizen sat on the bench inside staring at the wall, her hands held palm up on her knees.

Beyond the cell, Cassian walked up to a smooth stone wall, blocks cut so precisely they fit together with only hairline cracks.

"Here," he said. "I saw the magi working here."

Galin, the magi with the grown out military cut, joined him at the wall and ran her hands over the blocks. "There's no power here, now, but they could have moved the wall before the Darkness and left it completely mundane."

I held my breath as she closed her eyes to concentrate. If the food had been preserved magically, then nothing we did here would help save the settlement anyway. We'd open the wall and find nothing but dust and rot. This was a military installation, but there had been corners cut all around us. Like the bridge over the river and the roof of the barracks. Magic had slipped in everywhere, even when it wasn't supposed to.

Sweat broke out on Galin's brow, and she grunted. "I'm gonna need some help," she said. "I'm out of practice."

Helena and I stepped up and placed our own palms against the rough stone. I reached out to follow the lines of vytl the other magi had already drawn and matched my efforts to hers and Helena's. Together, we pulled at the crack where the wall met the ceiling. It grew wider and an entire section split away and slid forward with a rumble that I could feel through my worn boots.

We froze, and I glanced at the stairs with a wince.

No one came to investigate and the woman behind the bars just stared listlessly at the wall.

"I think we're all right," I whispered, and we turned back to the secret cache.

An opening half again as tall as Cassian had appeared, leaving just enough space on either side of the wall for us to slide through. My heart hammered as I shimmied through the opening. I sniffed, searching for the whiff of long-decayed food.

It just smelled dry.

I raised my hand to call light, but Galin beat me to it. A globe of yellow snapped into existence over her palm, lighting up her grin.

She laughed, breathlessly. "I'd forgotten the way that felt," she said. She pressed a hand over her heart, her smile flickering uncertainly in the light. "Should it feel so good? It shouldn't feel good. Not when it destroyed the world."

"Magic didn't destroy the world," I said quietly. "Misuse of magic destroyed the world. We shouldn't have to feel guilty about using every tool we have to survive."

I squeezed her shoulder before I turned to look over the hidden room revealed by our magic.

Intact crates lined the walls of a tiny space built into the hill. They still stood, held together by nails and glue. The air moved, cool and dry, to mingle with the fresh air coming through the opening.

My hands shook as I stepped up to the nearest crate.

What we found in here could mean the survival or the death of this community we'd built.

With a surge of power, I pried the lid from a crate. My breath released on a laugh.

Dried onions. Brown and flaky, with long, hairy roots, but pungent in the cool air.

Helena opened one next to me that contained strips of cured meat, and Cassian called out that he had barrels of dried corn and grain.

I put my hand over my mouth to suppress the relieved laughter bubbling up. This was it. This would help us survive one more year. Even with Titus nipping at our heels.

We ferried the stored goods into the main cellar where Decima would find them, and Galin and I closed the wall again.

When we finished, I gestured everyone up the stairs while I paused beside the cell.

I chewed my lip. I didn't know what I could do for the woman, but I couldn't just leave her here, beholden to Titus, wherever he was.

I wrapped my fingers around the bars and closed my eyes, trying to feel the wafts of vytl against my skin, learning the way they moved and the way they swerved around the woman before they were sucked into the vortex around her head.

Carefully, so carefully, I nudged the streams of vytl, prompting them to siphon off the swirling lines of light and direct them away from the woman. The power clung to her, sticking like river muck. I nudged harder, applying more to the problem, then brought my own power down like the edge of knife, severing its connection.

The halo of light sucked off with a slurp I could almost feel, and suddenly, she blinked. Her eyes went wide and clear instead of blank, and she started at the sight of the bars and the crates stacked around her.

"What—" she said, but I was already disappearing up the stairs.

The next day, there were rumors all over the settlement that Decima had found a miracle in the guardhouse. Whispers said that the Allfather had taken pity on us and Cassian's morning prayer vigil's doubled in size overnight. Other whispers said that magi had magicked the stuff out of thin air, but no one could prove it. When my father looked at me, I returned his gaze, teeth set, waiting for his question.

But he never asked it.

CHAPTER FIFTEEN

The barracks looked much more like an administrative center now, with the large table and chairs and maps and notes hanging on the walls. We'd moved all the bunks out months ago to individual houses as our large family had split up and blended into the population.

"How are things down in the town?" Papa said, standing at the head of the table, hands pressed against the surface.

"Well," Decima said. "Everyone seems to be getting along finally. We haven't had any incidents against magi in weeks."

Or anyone thought to be a magi. My people were safe. None of them were foolish enough to let slip about their abilities.

"Keeper Cassian?" Papa said. "What about you?"

"No one has expressed any violence toward my calling or the people who come to my prayer meetings," Cassian said.

"And we have enough food to last everyone until spring," Papa said.

None of them looked at me, although I knew every one of

them guessed the truth. I could almost feel Helena's glance even though she sat behind my shoulder with the notes.

Papa opened his mouth, his eyes crinkled at the corners with pleasure.

The door slammed open, making us jump and turn. One of Decima's scouts hung on the doorframe, gasping as if he'd run from Leu'aline itself.

"Titus," he said as Decima slammed back from the table and came to catch one of his arms. Max took the other. "Titus is on the move."

I stood, my chair clattering against the flagstones, pulse rushing in my ears. "What did you see?"

"He marches on Namar with an army."

"An army?" Helena said, voice rising. We knew he'd been gathering people. We'd seen them in the countryside. But that had been one or two. Many of Decima's soldiers had served in the legion. None of them would have been spooked by a handful of hostile scavengers. This had to be more.

"Are you sure?" Papa straightened but remained in place at the head of the table.

The scout nodded as Decima and Max helped him to a chair. "Ran from the old farm at the crossroads," he said, naming a landmark half a day's journey away. "Warned Abele's family on the way."

I was already moving while my family gathered around the scout to hear the rest of his report. I slipped out the door and into the octagonal tower, lifting my skirt to climb the steps, one hand on the wall. On the platform above, I stepped up to the edge. Then I raised my hands and drew power, spreading it across the air in front of me like a perfect pane of glass in one of the old cities.

Within the circle of magic, colors swirled, forming pictures.

I squinted at the waves of winter-brown grass being crushed under the boots of a motley group of people. I recognized the crossroads the scout had named and the figure riding ahead of the troops. And I counted. Over and over I counted.

It wasn't an army like the Empire had defined army. But it might as well have been. Titus had managed to find and bind a couple hundred people to his will. Against Namar's population of seventy, Titus's force looked devastating. They'd be here by morning. And we'd be overrun by nightfall.

A step on the stone stairs behind warned me my father had arrived. He stopped at my shoulder and stared at the window hanging in the air, picturing our destruction. I waited for him to tell me to take it down.

"Where would he have found all these soldiers?" he said instead.

"Anywhere," I said quietly. "He didn't have to convince them to follow him the normal ways. He just had to find them and take control of them."

A long moment followed where all I could hear was his breath coming steady and deliberate in my ear.

I'd freed the young woman from Titus's control. Could I do it again, on this scale? Definitely not. I'd have to concentrate on each soldier individually. Even if I got every magi in

Namar to work with me, we'd never get to all the fighters in time to save the settlement.

And if Titus was coming with the device, he could just convert more of us to his will. Maybe that's what his goal was. To take us over without even a fight.

More silence, but I could almost hear him thinking, planning. Calculating each variable and inevitability the way I counted crates and barrels of food and mouths to feed.

"We'll meet him as he comes," he finally said. His voice had gone cold and brittle. "Every fighter we have will defend this place, while the non-combatants retreat. We can protect them long enough for them to escape and find a new home."

I sucked in a frigid sip of air, but before I could respond he said, "You will go with them."

"What?" I spun to face him finally, but his expression remained fixed on the window in the air. "Papa, no. You need me with you. The device has to be destroyed."

"You aren't a fighter. I don't want you to be in a position where you'll have to make the choice to defend yourself. You'll go with the non-combatants and start a new home somewhere out of Titus's reach."

I flung my arms wide. "And where is that? Papa this isn't a battle we can retreat from. If Titus gains a foothold here, he's just going to keep coming, more and more powerful as he gains more and more people."

"What do you want me to do about it?" He seized my shoulders, and I worried for a second he was going to shake me. "You want me to send you out there to meet him? Do you want to be slaughtered by his soldiers? Or would you rather be slaughtered by our people when they find out what you are?"

"If it's going to be one or the other, then I want to choose the way I die."

His hands fell, but I couldn't find it in me to regret my words.

He swallowed, and his throat bobbed with it. Was his mouth as dry as mine?

"And I'm choosing for you not to die," he said, with that tone of finality every child knew from their father. "You're going with the non-combatants. I'm issuing the orders now."

He spun and started down the stairs before I could muster another argument, and I wrapped my arms around my middle, gripping the sharp points of my hips. The wind stung my cheeks, and I realized they were wet.

He was going to organize the defense and the evacuation. He would defend his people until he died. And he'd do the same for me. But all of our deaths were inevitable now. Even if I fled like he wanted me to, I would eventually die when Titus caught up. We'd all die if I did nothing.

But what would happen if I disobeyed? Could I save us all? Or would I just die like Papa said?

And would surviving be worth it if it meant I lost the family that was trying so hard to protect me?

Families raced across the trampled winter grass, carrying candles and torches and the very rare glass lantern. They passed me in the dark, heading across the river to the rendezvous point for our evacuation.

I trudged along, head down, hands holding my cloak closed, using the swirls and eddies of vytl to tell me where to put my feet. I could have asked anyone around me to use their light, but I wanted to walk alone, needed to walk alone for now.

At the entrance of the necropolis, Cassian stood in a pool of torchlight, ushering groups of children and other non-combatants into the dark tomb. I stopped before crossing into his light and watched. My fingers clenched in the fabric of my cloak. If I let go for a moment, I'd float away, as if only half of me occupied this plane. I had to hold tight to myself and my purpose or I'd fly off the face of Térne. Maybe I'd hang there, watching everything from above. Would I feel more complete up there among the clouds?

Cassian brushed his too-long hair back with an impatient hand before holding it out to a mother carrying one of her three children. The others looked on with tight jaws and white knuckles as Cassian murmured reassurances and then gestured them into the passage leading into the hill. The space beyond had been excavated in the years since we'd come, forming a wide cavern. It would be a tight fit for everyone but it would shelter us while Titus's force broke against the walls of the fort.

Cassian stood firm, directing each family, his hands steady, his voice calm. The planes of his face reflected peace and assurance to everyone arriving in the middle of the night.

He'd be expecting me. Papa had taken enough time to scribble our names on the job board under "Evacuation." But

Cassian didn't look up. He just continued doing his job. He looked good. Calm and collected in a way he'd been working toward for as long as I'd known him now. He didn't shake. He didn't avoid anyone's gaze.

He was himself. No one had forced him to be someone he wasn't. We'd respected his pain and given him the space and time to move on from it. And we hadn't pushed him to go faster. We hadn't forced him to be happy when he wasn't.

No one had drafted him into fighting against his will. He was here, protecting people the way he wanted to and the way he knew how.

He at least was complete in himself.

Unlike me. I hadn't been myself since the Darkness. Not fully. Not just because my family wouldn't let me, but also because I'd been afraid to be myself. I'd been afraid I'd lose them if I ever decided to actually be who I was.

I didn't know what I was going to do. But I knew I couldn't walk into that hole in the ground and pretend anymore. I couldn't keep living as someone I wasn't. Half a person.

Helena emerged from the necropolis entrance, her baby strapped to her chest to keep her hands free. She handed a blanket to the next family group to enter before she glanced up and saw me. Maybe she used vytl to see in the dark too and it had given me away. She caught Cassian's eye and gestured to me.

Cassian squinted, and I stepped closer. I didn't have to say anything. He saw my face and knew without words. Because he'd been through it all with me.

He gave Helena the torch and hurried over. He put his

hands on my arms and for the first time in hours I felt anchored and not ready to float away.

"I'm not staying," I said quietly.

He flicked a glance between me and the necropolis entrance. "I thought not. I'm all right here if you need to go."

I swallowed. "I'm done being half of myself. I tried. I tried so hard. But I can't anymore." I choked on the last word. The conviction felt paper thin, the edge of the Pit threatening to tip me back into the water again. What kind of monster was I that I was starting to hate my family for trying to protect me?

His hands tightened on my arms. "It doesn't make you evil, you know?" he said. "You can disagree with someone and still love them."

I squeezed my eyes shut and reached up to grip his elbows, holding onto his solid bulk. "But what if disagreeing with them makes me lose them?" I whispered.

"It might," he said with that calm implacable voice he used to answer every question. "You can't control how they feel. You can only choose how you react."

And I would choose to love them. Forever. Regardless of how they felt about me.

The thought rushed through my veins leaving heat in its wake. That was the constant to cling to. The anchor to hold me down. I loved them. I would always choose to love them.

It wasn't perfect. The choice I had to make was still awful and life-changing, but this anchor made the consequences of my choice one I could learn to live with.

"Thank you," I said, opening my eyes again.

He leaned forward to kiss my forehead, and I took the

opportunity to breathe in the smell of him, winter wind and damp earth and every steady thing I'd learned to treasure here in the heart of our new home.

"I'll see you after this is over," he said as if it was as simple as that. And to him it was. He'd see me when we won. Or he'd see me when we were dead.

"See you then," I said as he stepped away and his beloved features turned back toward the light and the job he had to do without me.

Helena faced us from the circle of torchlight, one arm wrapped around the blanketed baby. I didn't meet her eyes as I turned to rush back to the bridge.

CHAPTER SIXTEEN

I slipped up to the postern gate in the back of the fort wall, and with a touch of power, I made sure the guard above me didn't call out. Inside, I shut and barred the gate as the sun crested the eastern wall, sending glorious waves of gold across the stone walls. The light rippled across my fingers as I paused with my hand on the rough door, soaking up the slight warmth.

Along the top of the wall, Decima's militia stood, their weapons ready, their eyes trained on the east toward the crossroads where Titus was last spotted. Several of my magi stood with them, carrying their mundane swords and bows. The rest ferried water and arrows from the storerooms.

My family stood among them, backs straight, hands and eyes steady, every one of them. Papa and Mamma together above the gate, Max and Claudia flanking them. Decima, Valens, Quintes. Granmamma. Aunt Iulia and Aunt Priscilla. Dressed in their leather armor, uniform against the sunrise.

Uniform except for me. My heart clenched, and I swallowed against the hurt. This was the last time I'd be left out.

My father had raised fighters for the Empire. That didn't change just because there was no more Empire. How could he have missed the fact that he'd raised me to be a fighter, too? He'd made me. He'd taught me. And he'd Tempered me when he'd sent me to the Forge.

If he hadn't realized it, I'd just have to show him.

I stepped to the center of everything we'd built and sent a breath of wind to touch his cheek, just enough to make him turn with his brows drawn down. He caught sight of me, standing tall and still in the courtyard.

His shoulders jerked and his lips moved. Probably a curse but I couldn't tell from here.

He made for the stairs down to the flagstones. Mamma followed and as they abandoned the wall, the rest of my family turned to see.

I raised my chin as they stalked toward me. Above us, Max and Claudia exchanged a look.

"Aurelia, what are you doing here?" Papa planted his boots two feet from mine. "You have your assignment. Get back to the necropolis."

"No," I said. The tremors that had shaken my limbs the whole night, bled away, leaving nothing but cold calm. I couldn't remember if I'd ever said no to his face. "I'm here to do what I'm supposed to do."

My siblings climbed down from the wall with wary looks to join us on the flagstones. My magi remained motionless beside Decima's guards, but their gazes were sharp on my face.

Papa cast a glance around him as if to catalog who was listening. He knew what I was going to do. He couldn't have missed the inevitable slide of our conflict and where we would end up.

He took a small step and lowered his voice. "Aurelia, not now. Not here."

"If not now, then when?" I said, flinging out my hands. "When you're all dead?"

I reached across the space and pulled Max's sword from its scabbard. It was a mark of my brother's surprise that he let me.

I held the blade out level. My wrist ached, but I didn't let it tremble as I met my father's eyes. "You taught me that this is a tool. You taught me not to be afraid of it. The threat is only in the one wielding it." I let the blade fall and spun the hilt in my hand until I could offer it back to Max. "Magic is a tool. And I'm the one wielding it. Are you so afraid of me that you won't let me be who I am?" Max took the hilt from me, keeping his gaze on my feet.

Papa held my eyes.

"I can't be who you want me to be," I said. "I'm a fighter. I'm a Namarus. And I'm a magi."

I took several long moments to meet each of their gazes in turn. Mamma, Granmamma, Aunt Iulia, Aunt Priscilla. Max, Claudia, Valens, and Quintes. Papa.

"I love you," I said and stepped forward, around Papa.

"You're right," he said as I reached his shoulder. "You are one of my children. Which means you should know I would never send one of you out there alone but for your sword."

"Not alone," Helena's voice said from behind me. "But

you would send a commander out at the head of their division."

We turned in unison to see Helena standing in the courtyard, the ragged sling hanging empty across the front of her gown. The guard above the postern gate glanced over his shoulder and did a double-take when he saw us in the center of the fort. He was the only one not already watching us. Everyone else stared, waiting for something.

"Helena?" Max said, his brows drawing down in confusion.

She stepped forward and pulled the sling from around her neck to hand it to him.

"Where's the baby?" he said.

"She's safe with Cassian," she responded. She put one hand on his shoulder and leaned in to kiss him, then stepped back, her mouth going firm and flat. "And I know you'll keep her safe after this."

Max drew in a sharp breath. "Helena?"

A whistle from the guards above the gates made us jump. "Enemy in sight!"

Helena threw off her cloak.

I gulped, my stomach twisting, but I would never tell Helena she couldn't make this choice.

She met my eyes and nodded, no hint of regret in her gaze.

I unclasped my cloak as well, then I reached out to the power of the world and pulled myself into the air itself, traveling along whirling lines of vytl.

The old magi of the Empire had used the same power to transport thousands of troops across the countryside. But without practice and without the support of other magi, I could only manage myself.

With a bang, I landed outside the gates and tripped a couple of steps. Helena appeared beside me, feet planted.

I huffed a little laugh. Having an uneven gait didn't matter when I could just appear wherever I needed to go.

When I'd righted myself, I glanced up to see the horizon dark with Titus's forces. Hundreds just as I'd seen in the window the day before.

Helena and I exchanged a look.

"This is probably a really bad idea," I said with a desperate chuckle.

"No worse than theirs," Helena said, cocking a thumb over her shoulder at the fort defenders.

I didn't want to turn and look. To see my father standing there, watching me disobey him. I'd already thrown away the safety and security he'd tried to give me.

There was another crack of air, and Renallius stepped smoothly across the brown grass. "That used to be so much easier," he said, with a little shake of his shoulders.

Another crack and then Galin, the magi with the grown-out hair cut, appeared beside him.

My mouth dropped open with each successive boom until the valley was filled with the thunder of magi making up their minds.

I swallowed, surveying every single magi of the settlement as they stood arrayed against the walls of the fort. My chest swelled, and I bit my lip.

My own division of magi.

Renallius rubbed his hands together. "Concentrate on

taking down Titus," he said. "He's the one controlling them. If he goes down, the magic will most likely go out of them."

Galin said, "Avoid hurting anyone permanently. It's not their choice to be here."

Helena set her feet, one slightly back as if to prepare for a sprint. Then she glanced at me. "We'll clear a path for you. Get to Titus. He might still listen to you. End this."

I turned away from my magi, facing Titus's forces and planting my boots like Helena. For the first time since the Darkness, I took a deep unfettered breath. Complete.

Yes, something inside me said.

I raised my hand, then dropped it. "Go."

CHAPTER SEVENTEEN

It was no wonder strong men broke down crying on the battlefield. This mess, this noise, this chaos was about to cut through all of my carefully cultivated courage.

Titus's soldiers wore bits and pieces of old Empire armor, the bits that hadn't disintegrated completely. They moved toward my magi with a wooden sort of steadiness and we dodged them easily. But they moved inexorably, ignoring every wound and obstacle in their way.

The battle magi threw fire, blew holes in the ground at the enemy's feet, used their power to slice through swords one by one. But still Titus's troops marched forward, faces set. They kept coming.

But we were at a disadvantage. We didn't really want to hurt mindless puppets but the mindless puppets had no compunctions about hurting us.

A wall of enemy soldiers on my right fell, their feet tangled in a bright magic cord that pinned them to the ground, and I recognized Helena's handiwork. I sprinted on as the ground on my left heaved and bucked, trapping a group of the enemy behind earthen walls. Ahead of me, Titus's troops leveled their weapons to meet my charge until suddenly they were thrown backward, and their limp forms flew out of my path.

I raced for the opening, gaze sweeping across the battlefield. The enemy fought with an eerie silence, their mouths twisted in identical scowls, but there was still plenty of noise from the magi and from the creak of weapons and armor.

But where was Titus? I'd assumed he would be here to oversee his first mighty battle, striding out front with his head full of stupid notions of glory. I hadn't realized how hundreds of faces would blur into a constant sea of aggression. I skidded to a stop and took a precious moment to focus.

The device. Titus would be with the device. And every single one of these soldiers had a connection to it, one I could follow.

I squinted at the nearest enemy before he was flung backward by a rolling piece of earth. The vytl swirling around their heads had a definite pattern as threads of power swept away, toward the back of the vanguard.

Somehow I wasn't surprised he skulked behind the men and women he'd chained into dying for him.

I followed the threads, sprinting when the way was clear, ducking and dodging when it wasn't. Through the press of bodies, I caught a glimpse of familiar gold-tooled leather that made me stumble, but it was swallowed quickly by the endless figures around me.

A soldier lunged, his blade sweeping in an arc toward me, and I danced away too slow. The tip of his sword scraped across my cuirass, leaving a deep scratch in the leather. He lurched as if to grapple with me, and I reached out to pull myself along the lines of vytl, snapping out of his reach with a bang of magic.

I turned with an outstretched hand to bring my attacker down, but another figure beat me to it.

Max leaped on the soldier, taking him out with a smooth strike. My brother slashed out to flick the blood from his sword, frayed gray fabric swishing from the shoulders of his uniform. Helena's baby sling. He wore it like a cape.

I braced myself, waiting for him to turn on me and order me back to the fort. Or drag me there himself if he was determined enough.

Instead, he flashed me a reckless grin. "What are you standing there gawking at?" he said. "Get your ass moving and get to Titus. We'll guard your rear."

Behind him, Decima lunged to intercept another line of soldiers. Even farther back I caught a glimpse of Claudia's bright hair.

They weren't here to argue. They were here to protect me while I did what I had to do.

He shot me a quick salute as I raced back into the fray.

My magi pushed back the enemies at my sides while my family fell in to guard me from the rear, and I pressed forward, finding gaps, creating my own when I couldn't find them. The threads of vytl led me deeper and deeper until I finally found the edge of the battle where Titus lurked.

Four hulking soldiers surrounded him and a beat-up wagon, and he ducked, eyes bulging as his bodyguards went flying back. He stepped forward, putting himself between me and a battered box sitting in the wagon bed.

"Titus," I called, my voice rough but steady. "Stop this, now."

His features twisted, and he launched himself at me, fingers outstretched and glowing with magic.

I lifted a hand to block him and he hit a solid wall of power with a flash of light. He stumbled back with a cry, and I pressed the advantage, lashing out at him.

He tried to form his own shield and managed to deflect the worst of my blow. But I'd been practicing with real magi for the last few months. Magi who had been battle-hardened. Who had earned their ranks on the battlefield fighting other magi.

Titus had been playing with toy soldiers in comparison.

I threw him across the wagon bed. He crashed through the box and over the other side to land in the grass.

There, clamped to the wagon bed was the device. The box had only been there to protect it from prying eyes. Valens had already demonstrated that the delicate-looking glass couldn't be destroyed by normal means.

It looked so incongruous. A sweeping spiraling crystal flower of the old Empire clamped to a dirty wagon, wood splintered from its travels. The threads I'd followed from the soldiers all combined here, traveling down the petals to pool in the stem of the device. At its heart.

I clamped down on the gasping breath that wanted to escape my lungs and glared at Titus. "Stand down," I said. "I don't want to kill you, but I will if you keep threatening us."

"You're ruining everything," Titus screamed, pushing himself to his feet.

"Funny, that's what I was thinking," I said, planting my hands on my hips. I didn't look behind me, trusting the magi and my family to keep anyone from interfering. "We have the chance to build something new without the shadow of the Empire hanging over us. And you keep trying to drag us back there. We have to start as we mean to go on, Titus. And that means leaving our mistakes behind." I'd told Papa the same thing when we'd taken in the first refugees that would form our community. We couldn't keep looking over our shoulders.

"You think it's a mistake, but I think it's what the world needs. It needs order. It needs power and leadership."

"Not the way you think it does."

"You're destroying it all!"

"No. You're defending a past that deserved to die. I'm protecting the future that deserves a chance to live."

As Titus gaped, I drew all the vytl from the surrounding area, as quickly and smoothly as I could manage without burning myself up from the inside, and shoved it all into the device, pouring it down the sweeping glass petals into its heart. I force-fed it power until it was engorged, pulsing with a sick, yellow light.

Titus screamed and threw himself on the glass structure just as it swelled.

I flung up my arm as the device exploded in a shower of molten glass and the world went up in a brilliant, blinding flash of light.

CHAPTER EIGHTEEN

"——Stand back. It could be a backlash reaction," someone said through the ringing in my ears. "She could hurt you without meaning to."

I shook my head, both to answer the unseen speaker and to try to clear the cobwebs from my thoughts. But I shouldn't have moved. I couldn't see anything of the world, only a bright unwavering light, but the earth under me spun as if it was trying to fling me from the surface of the planet itself.

"Not backlash." I groaned and rolled over so I could cling to the dry, dead grass. As if that would help. "I think I hit my head."

From Helena's descriptions, backlash wouldn't feel nearly this good.

I covered my eyes with one hand to try to force the spinning to stop and only kept myself from heaving by swallowing down the bile gathered in my throat. A hand pressed the space between my shoulder blades, a comforting weight anchoring me to the ground.

When I finally managed to blink and crack my eyes, the light had receded to black flashes at the edge of my vision. Afterimages from the explosion.

I stared around me and sucked in a breath. Bodies lay all over the battlefield, Titus's soldiers sprawled where they'd fallen. Either stunned, unconscious, or dead. I hoped not dead.

Helena's face ducked into view. From the angle, it must have been her hand on my back. "How are you feeling?"

"Dizzy," I said. I gritted my teeth and pushed up to my hands and knees. From there, I managed to climb to my feet. Bits of cooled molten glass rolled under my boots. A few feet away, Titus lay on his back beside the wagon, bloody and still, his eyes fixed on the clouds above. Renallius knelt beside him, checking for any signs of life. He glanced back at us and shook his head.

Either he'd had some sort of connection to the device that killed him when it had been destroyed or he'd been too close when it exploded.

I pressed the palm of my hand over my heart and squinted around the rest of the battlefield. My magi waited nearby, some lingering to see if I was all right, others checking the bodies of the soldiers. Beyond their protective circle, dozens of figures from the fort gathered. There were many in gold-tooled leather among them.

I wanted to explore that avenue a little more thoroughly but something made me pause. In the last three years since the Darkness, I'd gotten used to the little bits and flashes of light and vytl moving through the world. Power I could see and touch and hear as whispers moving across my skin.

It wasn't there.

The entire battlefield was devoid of power. It lay bare and stark as if the color had leached out of it. It looked just like it had during the Darkness.

I gasped and looked up, checking for the sun. But it still hung there shining and making my eyes water.

"What's wrong?" Helena said, placing her hand under my elbow to steady me.

"The vytl. Where did all the vytl go? I poured it into the device to destroy it, but did I use it all? Will it ever come back?" There'd been a time when that wouldn't have been so bad. It would have solved at least some of the problems of being a reluctant magi. But now it would feel like a piece being ripped out of me, leaving me broken again.

Renallius took the chance to step forward, chuckling. His mirth immediately made me relax a bit. "It's only temporary," he said.

"Lots of battles between magi left the world looking like this," Helena said. "The vytl just needs time to replenish itself and disperse back into its natural channels. Look." She pointed. "It's already coming back."

I followed her gesture to see little flickers of color floating down from the sky. The same vytl I'd used to destroy the device scattered and now returning to gather in pools and rivulets around us.

"Helena," a voice called and the two of us turned to see Max hurtling across the battlefield. He didn't stop at the wall of magi like the rest of my family. He burst through and hit Helena running, lifting her into the air to swing her around. Helena laughed, a mix of relief and desperate joy in her voice as he peppered her face with kisses, making it very clear how much he cared that she was a magi. They spoke over each other in their haste.

"Don't scare me like that again. Why didn't you tell me?"

"I didn't want you to know. We didn't want anyone to know."

"Next time you want to fight, at least give me some warning."

The rest of my family used this excuse to move closer, past the line of protective magi. My sisters glanced at the surrounding destruction while the rest of my brothers spread out to join the magi who were checking the downed soldiers. Papa very deliberately stepped up to stand in the open space directly in front of me. The gold in his uniform glinted in the sun and he still carried his sword in a loose grip.

I licked my lips as Papa met the eyes of each magi in turn, cataloging them. Remembering their faces. They stood firm in the light with nothing left to hide them. This was the moment that would decide what kind of future we were building. Would it be one with magi? Or one without?

"Thank you for your service," Papa said, voice quiet but strong. "You've saved us all." He glanced at me. "Any casualties?"

I shook my head, a little stunned. "Not for us. What about you?"

"None. Your mother and grandmother I left in charge of defending the fort. A wing of Titus's army made it around to start attacking the walls but they all fell unconscious when you destroyed the device."

"Some around the edges have started to wake up,"

Claudia said from behind Papa's shoulder. "They're confused but at least they're aware of who they are."

"We'll need a plan to deal with the newcomers," Papa said. He took a moment to survey Titus's body and the bits of glass strewn on the ground. He knelt to pick up a piece and ran his thumb over the smooth surface.

"I'm sorry," he said. Then took a deep breath and raised his chin to meet my eyes. "I'm sorry I ever made you feel like you couldn't be yourself." He swallowed. "I thought I was protecting you. I didn't realize I was stripping a soldier of their weapon."

He knew. He knew who I was. Who he'd made me to be. And he was all right with it. He'd apologized.

I stepped into his arms and he closed them around me tight enough to squeeze the breath from my lungs, but I didn't mind. He rested his chin on my head, and his stubble scratched my scalp through my hair.

I sniffled, but within the circle of his arms no one could tell, and I made sure my eyes were clear before I finally pulled away.

"I don't want anyone to have to be afraid of who they are," he said, raising his voice so all my magi and my family could hear. "Will you help me build a place where we're all safe?"

"Yes," I said around the lump in my throat. "I will."

CHAPTER NINETEEN

*Y*es, fear is an ever present thing. New worries are always there to crowd out old ones.

But hope is there as well. That is why we keep living, keep fighting, keep building. I can laugh now, at my maudlin ramblings, because the outcome proved hope was the stronger of the two.

But it was only stronger because I made it so. I clung to it so it wouldn't be snatched away; I fed it with certainty and stubbornness and a little bit of anger.

If we are going to thrive, we will need hope as our weapon and our shield, and I will continue to make mine stronger, to guard it for the future.

The air had been warm again for nearly a month. The grass on the distant hills waved green in the sunlight, and Claudia and her people guarded the little green shoots sprouting up in the fields.

I stopped on the packed dirt road and closed my eyes, letting the breeze move across my cheeks as the hum of voices and construction pressed against my ears.

Of course, the influx from Titus's people had sparked a rush of expansion and trade. But I hadn't expected the noise of it. The almost constant chatter of human beings living their lives. The dull roar when they all gathered outside the fort to hear announcements or discuss the new policies Papa posted outside the barracks.

I started walking again through the market that had sprung up along the main road leading into the fort. Family groups that had traveled miles to find us and scavengers from the surrounding hills gathered to haggle over the first foraged fruits and vegetables of spring and the rarer luxury goods Valens and Quintes's teams had brought in. People trickled in once a week, having heard about us from neighbors and friends and travelers.

The majority of Titus's army had decided to stay with us. Some had slunk off, back to whatever hard existence Titus had dragged them from, but most were thrilled to have a place in our community. That had meant a lot more houses and buildings springing up overnight. And with practice, these were starting to look more like deliberate architecture, rather than hovels cobbled together with whatever we could find.

I waved to Renallius who supervised a group of magi raising the walls of a house beyond the market stalls. With that unique balance we'd been working on since the battle, the magi held the frame in place with magic, while the workers darted in with hammers and nails.

There were only one or two sidelong looks from the workers, but the rest worked amiably beside the magi. It helped that Ranallius himself went through and made sure the structure was sound before he signed off on it. Nothing in Namar would be held together by magic alone. The magi made sure of that.

Magic was a tool, not a foundation. But it also wasn't something to be afraid of.

After the battle, everyone was a lot more willing to see magic used around them. Most of the fort's defenders had watched the magi risk their lives and their place in our community to keep Titus from destroying us all.

That goodwill was backed by very real law now. Laws against assault and persecution. Very few settlers wanted to risk exile just to turn their noses up at magic, and those who did...well, we asked them to leave. Politely and officially.

I spent a lot of nights wondering if I'd just let Titus build something like this, using magic to help lift and carry and dig, would that have prevented his mad scheme?

Probably not. Titus seemed like the type to reach for more than he could hold no matter what. But I could have given him the chance to prove otherwise. If I hadn't been so afraid.

Now he was dead and he would never have that chance.

I chewed my lip as I dodged a group of strangers. They stared at my cuirass and whispered. Word traveled fast that the Namarus family all wore the leather uniform.

We needed a new name for the magi. The old word had

too many negative connotations. For both the magi and for everyone else. We needed a new name for this new time. Sorcerers? Wizards? Enchanters? Hmm, I'd have to work on it.

Just off the main thoroughfare, Cassian stood with his hands on his hips, squinting up at the front of his new chapel while Valens and Max pounded nails into the roof.

I sidled up next to him and put my arms around him. "It looks great."

"Almost done," he said, beaming at me.

It was square and squat and looked nothing like the massive temples for the Allfather and His pantheon that survivors of the Empire were used to. But I liked this better. The deity felt closer somehow in this humble building than He had in soaring towers and intricate stained-glass windows. And since one of the magi had cleared out the debris from the sawmill downriver, the siding even looked sleek and practical.

"Is it done?" Helena said, coming up next to me and shielding her eyes. She held my niece on her hip, who gurgled and held out her hands to Max.

He slid down the ladder. "Hey baby," he said, tickling his daughter. "The outside's snug and sound, Cassian. We'll need to build you an altar, but you can start holding services if you like without worrying about getting rained on."

"Thank you," Cassian said, his eyes never leaving his new building.

"And that means we can start on Cassian and Aurelia's house," Valens said with a smirk.

"Right next to ours of course," Helena put in, nudging me in the side.

"I'll bet it'll be really nice for you two to get out of Mamma and Papa's house." Max waggled his eyebrows.

I did not give him the satisfaction of blushing. I just hummed in agreement.

"Yes, your father snores," Cassian said, still admiring his chapel. "I haven't slept very well since you all arrived at the fort."

I rubbed a smile from my lips as my brothers gave Cassian an incredulous look. Cassian and I were together, yes, but I couldn't figure out how to explain that our together looked a lot different from everyone else's together. And frankly it wasn't any of their business, so I didn't have to. We had a comfortable sort of relationship built on trust and affection. Love of a different sort from Helena and Max. But that was as far as it went. And that was as far as we both wanted it to go.

It wasn't like Namar wouldn't be swimming in babies come next year. Papa would have plenty of grandchildren to teach how to be soldiers. We didn't have to contribute unless we really wanted to.

I squeezed Cassian, and he squeezed back before I stepped away and continued out past the outskirts of our new town. I held my skirt free of the damp grass as I trudged up the nearest hill where I could turn and survey what we'd built. In a moment, I'd go back. I'd take my lists and start assigning magi where they could do the most good without overtaxing them or making anyone else nervous.

But for now, I wanted to just look.

I huffed a laugh. Namar looked like nothing more than a collapsed anthill with all the insects busily trying to ignore the damage and rebuild. But I knew what you couldn't see on the surface. The love and the thought and the effort that went into each nail, each board, each hammer blow.

Three years ago, the fort had stood empty except for one lone man under a dark sun. Now it was home to hundreds of family members, neighbors, and friends.

I blinked as the view grew fuzzy and wavered. I raised my hand to my face and rubbed my eyes until everything settled and I stared out at a city stretched out in place of our fields.

I caught my breath. Buildings sprawled across the horizon, houses, temples, other things I couldn't identify, all with an architecture that didn't look anything like what had stood at the height of the Empire. Those had been filled with an ethereal, gilded beauty. This city was square, solid, built to last the ages. It wouldn't fall to anything easily.

The broad blue band of the Lirein split and snaked through the city in thin strips too numerous to count. A chapel with white spires gleamed in the sun, dominating the scene. And opposite the fort in a crook of the river, stood a blue palace, the seat of someone and something important and lasting. A dynasty to carry on.

A touch on my shoulder startled me. My balance faltered, and the vision faded as I stumbled back.

"What do you see?" Papa asked, hand still gripping my shoulder.

I rubbed my eyes again and stared, but nothing remained except our small houses and fields, Cassian's chapel, and the dirt path leading up to the fort.

Had it been my imagination? Or something else with a little bit of magic in it? I wasn't sure. Maybe one of the magi from the Forge would have been able to tell me, but I didn't need the answer. I knew what it was, regardless.

"A promise," I told Papa. A promise that we were building something strong and lasting.

And it was time to go back to work.

The *Mark of the Least* is a series designed to be read in any order, but if you enjoyed getting to know Aurelia and her family, you will love seeing another magi come into her power in By Winged Chair.

And if you'd like to read a short story about a phoenix and a fish sandwich, sign up here to get Rising, an exclusive *Mark of the Least* short.

THANK YOU FOR READING

Thank you so much for choosing to spend time with Aurelia and her family. If you loved this book, consider leaving a review so other readers can find more stories about heroes who can't run or jump or swing a sword but still manage to save the day spectacularly. And if you do, be sure to share it with me!

Visit me:
https://www.kendramerritt.com/

ABOUT THE AUTHOR

Books have been Kendra's escape for as long as she can remember. She used to hide fantasy novels behind her government textbook in high school, and she wrote most of her first novel during a semester of college algebra.

Kendra writes familiar stories from unfamiliar points of view, highlighting heroes with disabilities. Her own experience with partial paraplegia has shown her you don't have to be able to swing a sword to save the day.

When she's not writing she's reading, and when she's not reading she's playing video games.

She lives in Denver with her very tall husband, their book loving progeny, and a lazy black monster masquerading as a service dog.

Visit Kendra at
www.kendramerritt.com

facebook.com/kendramerrittauthor

goodreads.com/kendramerritt

instagram.com/kendramerrittauthor

tiktok.com/@kendramerrittauthor

Made in the USA
Monee, IL
06 November 2024